A Beach Reed

CANDACE BERTINI

ISBN 979-8-89112-461-5 (Paperback)
ISBN 979-8-89112-462-2 (Digital)

Covenant Books
11661 Hwy 707
Murrells Inlet, SC 29576
www.covenantbooks.com

The Island

Jesper Hawthorne came rushing through Pressley's bright red front door, almost jumping with excitement. Her front door had a gold lion door knocker right in the center that clacked as he tried to slam the door shut behind him. He was wearing a tan leather belt bag around his waist. His "fanny pack," as Pressley referred to it, was always in front, opposite the "fanny," and she assumed that was for efficiency in accessing the items it contained. Jesper reached inside one of the packs' zippered pockets and eagerly thrust the crumpled document a bit too close to her nose.

"I told you! I told you!" he spit shouted. She closed her eyes and held her hand up gently between them as if to shield herself from the incoming.

She eyed him from a side glance, and along with a deep inhale, she responded, "What exactly had you told me?"

Jesper stood five feet four, and that was if he was wearing shoes. His hair was a frizzy mess of undefined color. Who knew what might be nesting there? His wide and super-white-bright smile drew attention away from the mess above his head that must be considered hair. This stunning smile overcame any other faults Jesper might have had and caused most people to have an instant positive reaction to him. He wore white tube socks with black flip-flops (a no-no in her way of thinking, and how could anyone keep scrunching their toes through those tube socks to hang onto flip-flops?). He was usually dressed in shorts that she thought seemed a bit too small, and today was no exception. The hair on his legs, oddly, did not solve the mystery of the color of what adorned his head. His T-shirt had a simple saying in large letters: "I guess, therefore I am." Jesper thought it was a funny take on the traditional philosophy "I think, therefore I am."

She had assumed through the years of their friendship that he had attention deficit hyperactivity disorder. She never questioned his clear intelligence; she was just keenly aware of his inexhaustible energy and propensity to seemingly be everywhere all at once. The question of whether he might have this condition flashed through her mind as she watched carefully for his response, but the thought left quickly as he replied. He stepped back and set the papers down. His shoulders dropped, and his palms opened toward her.

"How can you be so calm? Are you serious? What do you THINK this is? Oh, I can't even believe you're…" His head was shaking as he turned, looking about for any food morsels that might be on the table. His attention turned to some tea biscuits, grapes, and cheese on the table, and he leaned over to pluck food with his right hand while waving the paper vaguely in her direction. Heartily chomping, he turned back to Pressley and pointed his left index finger accusingly toward her, further crumpling the paper. He had started to wonder whether she could possibly be getting some cognitive decline, or was it just her odd sense of humor that made him wonder.

Pressley leaned back and crossed her arms for the show she was sure would ensue. He was never still or calm. She watched quietly as the various foods on the table quickly disappeared, one by one. Pressley remained mischievously silent, staring directly at him while deciding to let Jess, as most people called him, continue his rant if he so chose.

"You are not going to believe where I found this! And it's because of the key!" he said through a mouthful of food.

She thought to herself, *How does he not weigh five hundred pounds? I have never seen him refuse to eat, and he eats all the…* After a few swallows, Jess was about to begin again when Pressley interrupted.

"The crypto genius is waving a *paper* in my face. Paperrrrr… hmm, will wonders never cease?" she said in a purposefully droll voice, drawing out the *R*s and the *M*s. "Got any papyrus in that pouch of yours?" she ended, looking back to her open computer.

Pressley liked to think of herself as having kept up with the world, and she actually did use her computer, pad, and phone, but in reality, she was far behind current technology while Jesper was not.

As their friendship developed, he would patiently listen to her stories of "how it used to be" in return for the sense of family and belonging that she provided. When he became even slightly frustrated with her lack of desire to delve deeper into electronic technology or social media, Pressley enjoyed reminding him that if they were exactly alike, then one of them would be redundant.

Jess's arms hung at his side, with his left hand still clutching the crumpled paper. He found the closest thing to sit on, an old, craggy butcher block in the corner of her kitchen that gave him an authoritative perch. He alternated leaning and sitting on the well-worn antique butcher block while again extending the paper and waving it rhythmically while he talked. "Thanks for acknowledging that I AM a crypto genius. Okay, but seriously, we should do something NOW! I printed and copied this at the library, and I've saved it so many ways that it won't ever be lost!"

Peering above her cheap red-rimmed reader glasses, she closed the computer and turned toward him to take the paper. She began to examine it. The document seemed to be a deed of ownership to a parcel of island land. Pressley lowered the paper and stared at Jesper. She paused and took a sip of black coffee to allow time for him to process. "Have you mentioned to anyone else how you came to be in possession of this?" Pressley asked.

"Of course not," he responded, somewhat defensively. "This is between us only. Like we always say, between the two of us, we know everything, right?" He widened his smile.

This prompted Pressley to laugh while nodding in agreement. "Indeed, we do. Indeed, we do. And figuring out the next steps is part of the 'everything' that *I* know, right? Hmm. Alright. It's time to think about the next steps carefully. If this document is what it appears to be, you could have more of a claim to property here on our little land-tied piece of paradise than many people think."

They sat silently for a moment.

"I went back to the post office today and asked, maybe even begged, old man Harriss to give me any information, anything at all. He claims he knows nothing about it and can't recall anyone accessing that PO box during his entire time working there. And he has been there since before sand."

There had been rumors that Jesper's ancestors were among the earliest settlers in the area, and at one time, these ancestors owned essentially the whole island. He remembered from early childhood his parents' conversations about their heritage, but for whatever reason, they discussed this less as he grew—or perhaps he just retained less as he grew past adolescence. Jesper's parents both died unexpectedly in an automobile accident while returning to the island when Jesper was seventeen. That was nearly ten years ago.

Although he was not technically of legal age to live alone after their deaths, no one had pursued a challenge to him doing so. Even if they had wanted to exert some control or influence over the young man, he would soon be of legal age anyway.

"Well, my dear," Pressley said while looking directly at him. "Tomorrow is another day. I know you just arrived, but I am quite exhausted, and a good night's sleep will help us both think clearly so we can make some sense of this. Nothing will change before tomorrow. Off you go!" She made a flippant and dismissive wave of her hand toward the door.

Jesper was frustrated and anxious to take action, but he also knew that he, too, was tired and that Pressley was right. He folded the paper, carefully placing it back into his fanny pack (or waist belt, if you prefer), and headed outside. His usual mode of travel was a well-worn purple beach bike with wide tires, a transportation habit that likely kept his metabolism on track. It wasn't that he couldn't drive a car; he probably could.

He jumped onto the purple bike, flip-flops and all, and pedaled away from Pressley's home toward the far edge of what he considered his island. Actually, it wasn't an island in the technical sense because it did connect to the mainland, but most of the area was surrounded by water, so it was generally referred to by locals as "the island."

His bike passed silently by white egrets fishing in the shimmering marshy inlet reeds as the sun set behind their slender legs. He passed a beachside hotel called The Island Barrier that appeared to be about half capacity based on the visible cars parked in the garage underneath. He passed multi-million-dollar mansions with hissing sprinklers spraying gently onto their precisely manicured lawns.

The land was flat, and the view, expansive. Coastal and inland waterways were changing as the earth was ever changing. Jesper loved this coastal land. He appreciated it, respected it, and considered it his family.

He rolled onto his own tiny space and threw his bike to the side of the few crumbling, concrete stepping stones leading to his door. A gray, weathered bike helmet hung on a hook to the side of the front door, obviously having received little use; it never moved from its hook.

Jesper lived in the most modest, small blue home, one block back from the beach. Rows of beautifully manicured mansions, with a few scattered pastel stucco beach homes, lined the streets. His was definitely the humblest and seemed more out of place with each passing year.

The property was only a tiny piece of land, barely big enough for the house, but the value continued to climb because of the surrounding property demands. He had lived in this same small community his entire, short twenty-something years and learned early to fend for himself.

Builders and realtors had offered him above-market prices for the property since the day his parents were buried, but Jesper felt no amount of money would be an even trade for the only home he knew.

After his parents' deaths, he had sorted himself quite nicely in the little blue house. It wasn't any fun being called "hobbit" by some of the local surfing boys who seemed to have endless money and endless fun, but still, he had always held his own. The town had many people who acted kindly, and he made it a purpose to focus his time and energy on them. A piece of paper was lying on the oyster shell grounds near his front door. A heavy conch shell rested in the middle of the paper. He was certain it had not been there when he left. To be exact, it was not a true conch shell because most species of conch were not native to the area. It was a large shell whose original inhabitant was long since gone. The shell was dry and heavy. Jesper lifted the shell and inspected both it and the paper as he picked it up.

He was shocked to find the paper was a copy of the deed—the very one now securely in his fanny pack and the one he was certain no one else had seen. His eyes scattered around the corners of the document, looking for anything to disprove that this could be the same. His first thought was, *But I just reassured Pressley that no one else had seen this!* His face and shoulders dropped lower with each step he took toward the indoors, not removing his eyes from the paper.

Once inside, he put both papers side by side and cupped his chin. They seemed identical. His thoughts turned to the day he received the key and what had transpired since.

CHAPTER 2

The Post Office

Jesper woke up as usual on the couch with a strong coffee aroma and the sun shining directly into his front windows. The house had a bed, but he rarely used it. Making beds seemed such a waste of energy—after all, wasn't it going to be unmade a few hours after you spent the energy to make it up? The coffee was waiting because he did not think it was wasted energy to fill and program the pot nightly. In fact, he had created a handy app for setting the coffeepot's delayed timer whenever he chose to. No matter that the coffeepot had its own built-in timer, he had fun figuring out his own more complicated way to program the pot. His app even notified him when the pot was empty, but in his case, that was always. His habit was to empty and replace the grounds and to fill the container with fresh water before drinking the morning coffee. In this manner, the pot was always ready. He made coffee like soup. His coffee had about 30 percent milk and 20 percent sugar, sometimes more.

Pressley was concerned with the quality of the coffee bean, while Jesper's primary concern was quantity. Jesper enjoyed texting Pressley to tell her that her coffeepot was low before he paid a visit. He had convinced her to allow him to set up his apps on her devices. She had decided to allow this even though it wasn't something she understood or appreciated. Much of the time, she had not bothered to read his texts, and she was quite annoyed when he raised the issue.

"What? My coffee is not ready?" he would repeat, and she would shake her head and silently vow again that she would not let the pot run dry to avoid a repeat scenario.

Jesper's house was one of the first on the mail delivery route, so he received his mail early in the day. There were exceptions because Mr. Harriss was actually on his own schedule. This morning, Jess had seen Mr. Harriss put the mail into his mailbox just a short while ago. He set down his soup-coffee and opened the door, squinting into the morning sun. He took the short walk to the small, weathered mailbox, flip-flops crunching on the oyster shells beneath, and pulled out the contents. Oyster shell recycling was popular among islanders. Oyster reefs and habitat were dwindling, and the recycling seemed like a proper reminder. Jesper and many permanent resident islanders used crushed oyster shells in clever ways, including in their landscaping and art projects.

He sat down at the kitchen table to look through a pile of mail, fully intending to throw most of it away likely without even opening it. His usual habit was to take mail from the mailbox and toss it onto the kitchen table until he felt like opening any of it. He sorted through a flyer addressed to "resident," a political ad, a couple of coupons, and a pizza advertisement. A small, undersized brown manila envelope resting on the pizza ad caught his eye. There was no label or return address on the sealed envelope. There was no discernible mark or anything unusual about the envelope except for its contents. He turned the envelope over a couple of times to ensure he wasn't missing anything, and then he quickly opened it. Inside was a small key. Just a key—no note, no letter, no other contents.

The small key had the embossed number "12." It was times like this that he wished he had a roommate or girlfriend, or…well, he did have Pressley. He had immediately decided to consult her and ran out the door for Pressley's place without even brushing his teeth.

Pressley had examined the key carefully and listened patiently as Jesper breathlessly told her how he had found it among the morning's mail. "Could it be a key to a safety deposit box at the bank? Could it be a key to a safe? Maybe just some kind of joke or accidental delivery, like maybe meant for a neighbor? Well, what do you think?" he asked excitedly.

Pressley turned the key over, looking for any potential markings or numbers, and saw the "12" embossing.

"I just *know* this is important. I can feel it! I just know it is," Jesper insisted.

"What if it *was* meant for a neighbor?" Pressley queried. In response, Jesper cocked his head to the side while shaking it, and he made a clicking sound with his tongue.

"I am going to guess you are on the right track and that this key might belong to a bank or post office box," she said.

Jesper bolted upright. "Well, let's get to the bank and the post office then! What are you waiting for?"

Pressley sighed. "I think it's unlikely, dear, that the key would fit one of those PO boxes at the post office."

Jesper was having none of this and made it clear that he was going alone if she did not want to accompany him.

Mr. Harriss was a lifelong resident who knew everyone in the community and many in surrounding communities. Mr. J. W. Harriss was affectionately called either "JW" or "the old man" by everyone in the town, depending on your generation. Residents above fifty-something called him JW, while the thirty-somethings and younger knew him as "the old man." Mr. Harriss was well over eighty years old, yet he still managed the post office six days a week. He had a fading old, orange Jeep with a right-hand driver's side from which he delivered the mail weekdays to every resident and some-times on Saturday if he felt there was enough to deliver.

The postal district had byzantine layers of micromanagement understood by few. What was understood was that Mr. J. W. Harriss considered himself the post*master*. The citizens were used to his eccen-tric manners, and most people considered him a town fixture similar to the courthouse or the flagpole. They had ceased to see his unusual nature. He wore a captain-type hat with a shiny black visor. White hair clumps randomly poked from under the sides of the cap. He had an unkept white beard to match. Blondie, the town's primary hair stylist, was appalled by his appearance and had given up trying to groom him. Anytime Mr. Harriss was in view, she would eagerly mention to those within a listening range that she had nothing to do with his appearance!

As for Mr. Harriss's feelings about Blondie's services, paying someone to cut his hair seemed extravagant. His mother's old pinking shears did the job just fine.

They pulled into the post office parking lot and parked beside a neatly kept front garden area containing coastal azalea plants and bordered with dwarf mondo grass that, upon close observation, contained small, deep blue berries. Pressley admired any plant that provided blue hues because of their rarity. Less than one in ten plants has blue flowers, and far fewer animals are blue. The sky and the ocean boast blue, but nature reflects it scarcely.

The post office was empty when Pressley entered through the open, smudged glass door held by Jesper. "Good morning." Pressley smiled toward Postman Harriss. Jesper squirmed in anticipation of the real issue. He was occasionally irritated by her slow and deliberate manner. Why didn't she just get to the question immediately? "We seem to have found a small key," she said, glancing back at Jesper. On cue, Jesper squirreled into the leather fanny pack and plucked out the key. He handed it to Mr. Harriss.

Mr. Harriss was extremely nearsighted. He spent the day holding letters and packages as close to his face as possible. He wasn't aware that he contorted his face and squinted terribly just to read labels. His eye doctor was located in the city of Wilmington, but he rarely visited because the doctor's most recent advice was not something he chose to follow, and he certainly didn't want to hear it again. All his usual customers considered his collective behaviors to be endearing idiosyncrasies.

Pressley smiled again at Mr. Harriss. "We have found this key in Jesper's mailbox and are wondering if you might have delivered it yesterday morning. It came in this unmarked, small manila envelope."

Jesper blurted, "Do you remember if my mailbox was empty yesterday when you put the mail in my mailbox?"

"Yes, yes, I do. Of course, it was empty," he grumbled, clearly irritated. "And I don't deliver mail that ain't addressed properly, durn it. First thing I do ev-er day, ev-er box, I peep in there to make sure I know what's going on! Yes, I do! Of course, it was empty. Yes, it was empty…" He trailed off while holding the key about two inches from his face and squinting painfully in its direction. "And what's more, tamperin' with the mail by puttin' somethin' *in* or takin' somethin' *out*, now that's agins the law. I tell you. This here is a key, maybe to a box somewhere." He waved them off dismissively as he put the key down on the counter in front of them.

Undeterred, Pressley said, "Of course, you would know! That's why we came to you, JW. We trust you like no one else in this town. Absolutely, you would be the one person we could consult who would *definitely* know!" Pressley knew that Mr. Harriss's propensity was to feel underappreciated and overworked. She waited for the effect of her acknowledgment to settle in. This comment seemed to calm Mr. JW Harriss considerably.

Pressley continued, "You see, we noticed that one side is embossed with "12" and thought that might mean Post Office Box 12, so we naturally thought of you as the best expert to help us solve the mystery."

Mr. Harriss straightened his posture and said in his slang, "Oh, yeah, yeah. I seen the number on it. I surely did. We got a box with that number. Yes, we do, but I ain't never had anyone access that box, and I oughter know. Yes, sir, I oughter know." He picked up the key again and firmly pressed it back into Pressley's hand. He began to ramble, "I would know. I would know," nodding his head, agreeing with himself.

Jesper and Pressley stood patiently watching Mr. Harriss. Another customer had entered the lobby and quietly exited after mailing some letters through the local mail delivery slot.

"Well, ya see, we changed all them boxes out several years ago," he said while waving his right hand generally in the direction of the small "PO Box" section. Lemme look at the list. That box number 12 is one that ain't leased, lest that I kin recall, and I gotta memory. Yes, sir, I do. And nobody art to be near them boxes unless they have permission, ya see?" He squinted directly toward Jesper through thick-lensed glasses. Mr. Harriss turned his back toward them to shuffle through clipboards of yellowing lists surrounded by piles of old pencils, pens, and tape dispensers of various sizes. He scratched at his neck with one hand while continuing to move various objects around with the other.

"Now that there key, that key is from the *old* boxes, not these durn new ones ya see," he said, still with his back turned to them, waving his arm generally in the direction of the post office box area in the lobby.

Pressley smiled politely and glanced toward Jesper, raising her eyebrows. "Well, there would surely be no harm in us trying the key, would there?"

Before Mr. Harriss could raise his strong objection, Jesper had snagged the key from Pressley and sprinted to the PO boxes. He quickly found number twelve and was inserting the key before Mr. Harriss raised an arm and started toward him, saying, "No, no, now, here. See here. I have to give you a lease before you can—"

Before Mr. Harriss was able to finish his sentence, Jesper had inserted and tried to turn the key, but he did not find that it would open the small box. His facial expression reflected the disappointment he felt at the lack of access to the box and any potential contents.

Mr. Harriss said, "That there type key shouldn't open that there box, shouldn't even be able to insert it, now that's a fact, but I seen that it fit into the lock. Where did you say you got that key, young man?"

Pressley and Jesper exchanged knowing glances and thanked Mr. Harriss for his time. Jesper returned the key to his fanny pack. Pressley avoided Mr. Harris's question by reminding JW that he was always welcomed at her home for supper any time he found the time and that she would love to see him at church too.

JW was a confirmed bachelor, and even though it certainly wasn't the case, he assumed any woman older than forty was looking for marriage, specifically a marriage to him.

As they left the post office, Jesper was initially silent. They got into Pressley's vehicle and headed back to her house. Pressley owned a refurbished, mustard yellow Land Rover 90 with inward-facing rear seats.

"Next stop is the bank," Pressley said calmly.

"Why in the world would anyone give me a key that doesn't even open an old, empty box?"

Jesper mused, *That just doesn't make any sense. It must fit something, or it must be of some use. I don't get it.*

Pressley remained silent in thought as they drove toward the bank. Pressley looked as though she had lived her years. People usually judged her as being more stern than she actually was. She was of average height and weight, with gray hair arranged in a bun. She had a bit more means than the average person, but she was by no means wildly wealthy. She was, however, wildly practical. She pulled into the bank parking lot and parked.

Once inside, Pressley approached one of the seated bank employees and pulled out the key while Jesper patiently waited a polite distance away. Jesper saw immediately from the employee's response that they had hit another dead end.

CHAPTER 3

Blondie's

Jesper had gotten little sleep that night, unable to stop think-ing about the key that fate seemed to have placed in his mailbox. That next morning, he was eager to continue the conversation with Pressley and headed straight to her place. Pressley was kneeling and working thoughtfully with a rusty garden spade, intending to move a large chunk of purple and white pansies to another area in her side garden. She hadn't chosen the perfect spot when initially planting them.

Pansies added color, but only at cooler times of the year in this warm coastal climate. The low, delicate, brightly blooming flowers were a cheery sight. Although the flowers weren't spectacular during the dead of winter, in Pressley's experience, they provided fabulous spring blooms if left in the ground through the winter. They pro-vided welcome color against the varying shades of green and brown in her yard.

Four multicolored chickens meandered aimlessly within sight, pecking constantly. Pressley stood up and clucked her tongue, shak-ing her head from side to side. She turned to look at Jesper as he arrived, and she said, "What are you up to this fine morning?"

Jesper was anxious to continue their discussion of the key. He knew if he stayed very long, he would be holding the spade. While that thought crossed his mind, Pressley put the spade firmly in his hand and pointed between where the pansies bloomed now and where she wanted them to go. Pansies always benefited from dead-heading, an activity that energized Pressley but certainly not Jesper. Before she could speak again, he said, "You could have put those there in the first place, you know, right?"

She paid no attention as she threw her gloves into a small garden cart. "I will be right back with iced tea and maybe more," she said as her eyebrows went up, disappearing under the unraveling, worn straw hat.

Pressley's backyard was encircled by a black fence and had a garden shed that looked like a small version of her own home and a complementary-colored chicken coop. She had four hens but no roosters because the town would not approve and did not appreciate the regular morning alarm provided by roosters.

Pressley soon returned with tea and delicious homemade square shortbread biscuits. Jesper was making good progress on moving the flowers to their designated spot when Pressley announced she was leaving for a scheduled haircut and asked Jesper if he would be so kind as to throw some food to the chickens.

"But I want to talk about the key!" he said with urgency.

"Oh, of course, yes, but later, sweetheart. I can't be late," she said as she walked briskly out of sight, seeming to Jess to completely dismiss him.

He finished planting the pansies in their new spot and walked to the small, tidy garden shed that held tools and chicken feed. While Jesper scattered some sunflower seeds and corn, Pressley made a brief stop at the main grocery store and then drove to her scheduled haircut.

Blondie's Barber Shop was located on Main Street, directly in the middle of the small group of businesses that included two bars, several restaurants (depending on the season), a shaved ice shack, a store trying its best to provide groceries and general supplies, and Blondie's.

Blondie was naturally the owner of Blondie's.

Blondie's featured a small, rotating antique barber pole that served as a unique landmark for anyone biking around the island.

Blondie's father had been a barber in the area for several decades, and she had inherited both the shop and the barber pole.

She cut most everyone's hair, from the youngest to the oldest, from the hairiest to the baldest.

Blondie knew the townspeople's business, and she could recall a good bit of the seasonal tourist business as well. Blondie was good with business and with people. She loved animals and made sure that there was always a bowl of water out for any passing animal.

The water bowl rested on a mat that said, "Dogs welcome, people tolerated." People walking their dogs would occasionally stop to allow the dogs to lap from her free water offering, but there were no other "passing animals." The thought of passing animals was more Blondie's wish than reality.

Pressley was punctual and arrived at Blondie's exactly one minute before her scheduled appointment. She valued timeliness and detested habitual lateness; she thought it incredibly rude and potential evidence of incompetence. She had learned to be tolerant of Jesper's propensity for tardiness and considered him an exception.

Blondie wasn't fully booked today, and she welcomed a nice chat with Pressley.

"So you still insist on the bun under the hat? If you would just let me," said Blondie.

But Pressley would have none of that. "Just trim the gray mane and let me out of here," Pressley responded as she removed the beige canvas sun hat she was wearing.

Blondie was about five feet six with bright blond hair and multiple arm tattoos, and her eyes squinted shut when she smiled. She was dressed casually in fashionable jeans with no less than four rings, three necklaces, and large hoop earrings. Blondie was cheerful and entertaining to her customers and a genuinely happy person. No one left Blondie's in a bad mood.

"I've been to pay a visit to our own JW Harriss." Pressley offered this opening topic as Blondie pumped the chair to the proper height and wrapped the plastic chair cloth around Pressley.

Blondie's smile was so wide that she appeared to have her eyes closed, and dimples appeared on both sides of her face. "Oh, oh, oh!

He kind of reminds me of Mr. McFeely from the old Mr. Rogers show, remember him? But Mr. McFeely didn't have hairs coming out of his *nose* and *his ears*!" She laughed heartily, dropping her scissor-wielding hand and shaking her head. "That man is in his own world and always has been," said Blondie.

Pressley couldn't disagree with that observation. She smiled while listening for more.

"I thought he cut his hair with a weed whacker, and I can-*not* believe it's actually an old pair of pinking shears. Did you know that? I can't remember who told me that." Blondie continued as she focused on Pressley's head and began to cut her thinning gray hair.

Pressley was deciding whether or not to share information about Jesper's key when Mr. Douglas Dyer came into the shop to notify Pressley that an antique they restored for her was ready for pick up. Douglas Dyer was the owner of The Antique Shop, which was across the street and "catty-cornered" from Blondie's. Mr. Dyer had obviously been jogging, which was his daily habit.

"I thought that was you, Ms. Pressley. We've got that antique ready, and please excuse my appearance, ladies!" he said, looking at Pressley in the mirror she sat in front of. "And morning, Ms. Blondie! Stop by and pick it up at your convenience." He continued looking at Pressley.

"Dorothy wanted me to catch you. She said she thought she saw you come in here," Douglas said, smiling while holding the door with one hand and waving toward them with the other.

Douglas was a genial fellow with a keen eye for a bargain. He prided himself on dealing fairly with customers, and he consequently enjoyed a good reputation in the area. His small dog, Anti, was lapping from Blondie's storefront water bowl. Anti was a brown-and-white terrier, a mischievous little lover of life who was always up for an adventure. Anti wore an old leather collar from which dangled a newer nametag with the store's name, address, and phone number embossed on it. Today, Anti was dressed up in a green scarf decorated with sailboats and oars. Most people thought the dog's name was "Aunty." Her name was not Aunty, but *"Anti,"* which was short for "antiquarian," meaning someone who loves antiques. Douglas and

Dorothy had long ago grown tired of explaining what the dog's name really was, so they would smile and chuckle to each other every time someone asked whose aunt she was.

Douglas wished them both a good day and left with Anti and her jingling tag bouncing along closely behind. As Douglas was leaving, Jesper entered. Blondie smiled while feeling very hopeful that she might get an opportunity to tame the mass on Jesper's head.

"Oh, hi there, Jess. How about some coffee? Just help yourself," Blondie said cheerfully.

Before he could move the direction of the coffee, Pressley said, "Jesper, be a dear, please, and pick up the box that has the antique Douglas and Dorothy redid for me. Just bring it back here, and we'll put it in the car, or I'll come down to the shop after, and we can load it then. It may be heavy."

Jesper sighed; the coffee was in sight. He nodded, turned, and headed back out the door.

"Douglas sure is a nice man," Blondie said.

"Yes, he sure is," Pressley responded. Pressley transitioned abruptly. "We had something curious happen this morning."

"Really? What happened?" Blondie responded, beginning to snip strategically.

"Jesper found a key in his mailbox. That's the reason we paid a visit to JW. The key looked like it might belong to a PO box or a safety deposit box or the like." Pressley waited for Blondie's thoughts on the matter.

"Wow! That sounds like a cool mystery. What was in the box?" she asked.

"Well, that's just it," Presley replied. "The key didn't open the PO box, and Jesper is quite vexed about it."

"Interesting," Blondie said as she stepped back to view Pressley's head from other angles.

"That's a beautiful shell you have on the counter here," Pressley noted, making small talk.

"Thank you," replied Blondie. "I found it just a few weeks ago on my morning stroll."

Pressley knew that seashells have long been embedded in cultural meaning and lore. Shells in some Asian cultures are considered lucky, while many in Latin America consider shells unlucky. Most dream interpreters consider shells a positive sign of growth and good luck, and they are considered hopeful by some religions. Pressley did not begrudge the tourists their occasional shell collecting, but debate had been rising around the overall impact on the local environment from overcollecting the natural resource of shells. Tourists saw shell collection as a peaceful and harmless activity, and maybe it was, but some on the island did not agree with that view.

Blondie continued her snipping. "What did JW know about this key from the mailbox?"

"Nothing, no help at all," answered Pressley.

Blondie said, "That doesn't really surprise you now, does it?"

Pressley smiled. "No, no, it doesn't, but one has to start somewhere, and the bank and the post office seemed logical starting points."

Mr. Mitch Castinoff poked his head into Blondie's and asked if she could see him later today for a haircut. Blondie barely looked up from cutting Pressley's hair, and as she continued precise snips, she said, "Sure, come on back whenever you have time. I'm open most of the afternoon today. Of course, if someone else comes in, you may have to wait a bit."

Mr. Castinoff said, "Sure thing. Thanks much. I'll be back."

Mr. Castinoff was an attorney, and he was married to the owner of the local beach sundry shop called The Beach Reed. Together, they also owned a real estate business.

CHAPTER 4

The Antique Shop

Jesper entered The Antique Shop and approached Mr. Dyer while doing a 360-degree search of the place with his eyes. There was so much to see in this establishment! Mr. and Mrs. Dyer had operated the shop for many years and were well liked throughout the community. The shop included ice cream served from an old-fashioned chest freezer–type dispenser. They wisely positioned the ice-cream freezer in a clear view of the large, glass storefront. Mrs. Dyer had a small area for fudge making, and she generally always had chocolate and peanut butter fudge available.

The Antique Shop served as a second landmark because of the giant ice-cream cone mounted above the front door. Before Jesper could speak, Mr. Dyer welcomed him. "How about a fudge sample today, Mr. Hawthorne?" he cheerily called out.

Jesper's left hand rested on the fanny pack as he grinned and readily agreed. "I don't have any cash today though…," Jesper said, trailing off as he watched Mr. Dyer retrieve a healthy sample of peanut butter fudge from behind the counter.

"Your tab is good here. No problem. Besides, it's just a sample, remember?" Mr. Dyer offered with a wink and smile.

Jesper readily accepted the fudge and then recalled his reason for coming into the store. "Oh, I'm here to pick up something for Ms. Pressley. She wants me to take it down the street to where she is at Blondie's. We are going to load it into her car. This fudge is great! Thank you!" Jesper said.

"You are welcome, dear!" chimed Mrs. Dyer from somewhere unseen in the back of the store. Jesper noticed something in the right-side corner of the store that he wanted to get a closer look at. There it was, standing between and just behind two small dressers. It wasn't fully visible, but he could see that it was made of several neat rows of small metal boxes with numbers. He shoved in the remaining bite of fudge and called out to Mr. Dyer, who had wandered to the other side of the store.

Mr. Dyer called back, "I'll be right out. Just let me get the box for you."

Jesper's heart was pumping harder, and he could feel a jolt of adrenalin. "Okay, hey. Where did you get this set of little metal locker things? Is this what I think it is?" he asked, dropping his hands to his sides and leaning in.

Mr. Dyer came out carrying a large, heavy box. "Oh, that I think is a set from a section of old post office boxes. I don't remember if JW brought those in or who left them with us. Generally, it's my understanding that those can't be reused or resold, and I was surprised to get them. Probably fairly old. Let me ask the wife. Hey, Dorothy, do you remember who sold us the post office box set back here?"

Dorothy's walk reminded Jesper of one of Pressley's chickens, lumbering side to side to result in forward motion. Dorothy appeared, rocking side to side and with a pleasant smile. "Oh goodness! I certainly *should* remember, shouldn't I?" she said as she put her finger across her mouth and stared at the metal boxes.

Jesper could not stand the excitement and did not wait for Dorothy to recall the origin of the PO boxes' origin. "Do you mind if I try something?" he said as he fumbled the key from the fanny pack and leaned farther toward the boxes. Douglas had gone back to the front of the store to wait on incoming customers, and Dorothy patted Jesper's back as she made her way past him. "Whatever you want to do will be fine, I'm sure, and you need to be wearing a helmet when you ride that bike, dear," she said.

Jesper had not ridden his bike today but had instead walked to the business area of Main Street, but Dorothy knew him well enough to know that he never wore a helmet when riding his bike. Dorothy Dyer was quite safety-conscious and knew the statistics. Those who insisted on riding without helmets were at the highest risk for traumatic brain injury, and she couldn't bear the thought of that sweet young man, or anyone else, for that matter, being vulnerable. After all, accidents were not called "planneds"; they were called accidents for a reason.

Jesper could make out the number 12 on one of the boxes, and he fumbled nervously in the fanny pack for the key. The key worked! In the box was a piece of folded paper. He squeezed further into the tiny space in front of the boxes, anxiously took the paper out, and unfolded it. It appeared to be a deed to a parcel of land on the island. What was at the bottom of the paper was the most intriguing part. It registered clearly the names and dates of the purchaser, which caused him to stop breathing. Time stood still for a moment as his eyes became fixed on the bottom of the paper. His own parents' names were listed as the owners! He wasn't sure how long he had been looking at the paper when he heard a voice.

"Hey, Hobbit!" he heard as he snapped back with a clap to his back that almost knocked him over. "I didn't see your ride outside. You coming today? It's off the hook out there!" A young man with baggy red striped shorts who appeared similar to Jesper's age grinned. He smiled briefly at Jesper and was about to ask what was in Jesper's hands when a tanned, tall, handsome blond-haired young man approached, shaking his head and speaking only to the young man in the baggy red striped shorts.

"You know he's a kook. I wouldn't ride anywhere near this doofus," the blond young man said.

"Let's get outta here. We've got perfect weather coming in."

Jesper didn't lift his eyes from the paper, hoping the young men would leave. Two tanned young women with white shell necklaces and whiter teeth were giggling and chatting loudly and appeared at once, grabbing the boys by their hands and insisting they get outdoors and to the surf.

"Ice cream! Ice cream!" they both squealed, insisting that the boys had promised to buy them ice-cream cones.

"Later, Hobbit," said the first young man, whose name was Tanner. He paused momentarily as if he wanted to engage in conversation with Jesper, but at the girls' insistence, he turned back to walk to the front of the store toward the ice-cream chest.

Jesper waited patiently as he heard Mr. Dyer serve up the ice cream. Finally, he heard the door close behind the surfing crew. He carefully folded the paper and placed it and the key slowly into the fanny pack's open pocket, staring intently at the wall like a statue, deep in thought. He wasn't sure how long he had been motionless when he snapped back to reality and looked around. The proprietors, Mr. and Mrs. Dyer, were busy in other areas of the store, and Jesper left as quickly as he could without saying goodbye. He rushed across to Blondie's and burst through the door. A new customer was sitting in the chair Pressley had previously occupied. "Oh, hello, Jesper," said Blondie. She was so pleased that he recognized the need for a haircut that she wanted to make sure he didn't have to wait. Before she could usher him to a seat, he said, "Pressley. Where's Pressley?"

"Oh, she went home. She said if you came back to let you know she would be at home, and she would pick up the package later. She said you could leave it here, but I see you don't have it."

Jesper now remembered that he was supposed to have brought her package back to Blondie's, and he was slightly irritated that Pressley hadn't stopped at The Antique Store as he assumed she would. Jesper ran as fast as he could to his home to retrieve his bike.

CHAPTER 5

The Library

He wheeled up to the local library and, in one swift motion, dismounted and put the bike on the upright metal pipe pole stand. Putting the bike on the stand, his thoughts drifted to what it would be like to drive a car rather than choosing the bike.

Truth be told, Jesper did not ever want to drive and avoided the subject whenever possible. His parents had died while driving. It was difficult to avoid the driver's education course in high school, but a note from his physician had taken care of that. Some people called it a "doctor's *excuse*," but Jesper certainly didn't consider it an "excuse." The note came on the heels of the most embarrassing incident of his life (at least, the most embarrassing so far). He had reported for driver's education class along with the countless other students who qualified, but it was only he who had a terrifying panic attack as he tried to slide behind the driver's seat. He hated any thought or mention of it!

Jesper had been delayed in taking driver's ed for two reasons. First, his birthday fell just short of his being eligible for public school first grade, so he stayed a second year in kindergarten and entered first grade as one of the older children in his class. Second, he wasn't keen on driving during his teens because his bike took him anywhere on the island that he wanted to go. Traveling this way seemed so much less complicated than all the responsibilities that go with maintaining a vehicle.

During the panic attack, he thought he was certain that he was near death and was either having a heart attack or a stroke. His symptoms were severe and came on quickly. The fuss and the aftermath from the ambulance ride—the school nurse, the crying girls—how traumatic it had all been for him. It was Pressley who had come to collect him after he spent a cautionary night of testing in the hospital. The event had taken place only months after his parents' deaths.

Jesper walked inside the library, looking cautiously left and right. He had the distinct feeling he was being watched, and he could not relax while there was a seeming mystery to solve. Who could have had access to his mailbox? He responded to his own thoughts, *Anyone, of course!* There was the fact that JW had claimed Jesper's mailbox was empty when JW put the mail in, but not much time had passed before Jesper had collected it. Was there time for someone to insert the key without his seeing? And what about the key fitting the set of boxes at The Antique Shop? Why did the Dyers not readily recall exactly when they had received the metal boxes?

On the left side of the library was a small brick building that appeared to be a home but had been refurbished as the law office of Mitch Castinoff. The building was trimmed in sharp, white paint and had an arch-top entry door that gave the office a good deal of charm. Two people that Jesper did not recognize were coming out of the law office as he was entering the library.

Jesper's focus was on the door, and he chuckled to himself. "Hobbit indeed! Mitch Castinoff, now *there's* a real hobbit, and he has the front door to prove it!"

Overgrown nandina plants dropping their red berries were nestled between dwarf hollies on either side of the arch-top white door. On the right side of the library was a local florist and gift shop named Whiffy Bloomers. Janice Whiff was the owner of Whiffy Bloomers. The shop featured a large selection of gifts and was the town's main provider of flowers or plants for anniversaries, birthdays, and funerals.

Jesper took out the deed carefully, glancing around. The few people in the library seemed otherwise occupied, and no one seemed to notice him. The on-duty librarians were also occupied and did not take notice of him. Jess was quite familiar with the library and spent time there almost weekly. He took a picture of the deed with his phone and then laid the deed on the copy machine to produce two copies.

What old equipment, he thought, while trying his best to wait for the second copy of the paper. The copy machine was indeed terribly old and inefficient. He glanced over to the librarian's desk and took note of a stack of manila envelopes identical to the color and size of the one he had received in his mailbox. Was he noticing the envelopes because he had just received one, or was the universe pointing him to a clue? As he recalled his father saying with some frequency, it seemed a "regular curiosity."

He was aware that several large maps hung in the library, but he had not paid special attention to them until now. Jesper walked over to a sectioned map of the area and held up the deed, wondering exactly which plot this deed was referencing. He glanced back and forth between the two with his mouth agape, trying to calculate where the plot would be located today. He slowly let the hand holding the paper drop to his side as he determined that the deed seemed to incorporate property that included the shop known as The Beach Reed.

Jesper bolted from the library, almost knocking down Mrs. Dorothy Dyer, who was coming in. He apologized profusely, and after holding the door for her, he mounted the purple bike as quickly as he had dismounted it.

Back to Pressley's, he thought, *and we won't be gardening!*

CHAPTER 6

The Beach Reed

Since the evening that Jesper had burst energetically into Pressley's and shared the deed document with her, she had been thinking about the best way to deal with it without stirring up unnecessary gossip and rumors. (And just in case you are wondering, *yes, there is such a thing as "necessary" gossip and rumor!)*

Possibilities had been discussed: If they took the deed to Mitch or to Tara, wouldn't that be like poking a sleeping dog? Asking for trouble? Who should be trusted and consulted? Pressley ultimately decided the best course of action was to be as direct as possible.

"We are headed to The Beach Reed *and* to Mr. Castinoff's office," she said firmly.

Jesper jumped up from leaning against the butcher block in her kitchen. "What? But if we do that, he'll go straight to Tara, and they will do anything they can to disprove this document as fast as they can! There is no way that Ms. Tara will let anything happen to her store. You know that is her baby."

"My friend," she said, pausing to be sure she had his attention. "One truism that I have learned, if nothing else, is that all behavior has meaning." She had said this many times before. "Remember, Jesper, *all* behavior has meaning. There aren't many absolutes in this life, my dear, and the fact that all behavior has meaning is an important one. Let's see how they both behave when we show them your document." Pressley smiled. "That will tell us much more than any words that they use."

Pressley needed a new straw hat to keep the sun from further damaging her already-weathered face. They rode up to The Beach Reed store in Pressley's yellow Land Rover. The store didn't appear to have many customers. It was a particularly hot day without any clouds, and the bright sun was producing a shiny glare coming from the *B* in The Beach Reed sign. Jesper looked around, wondering if there was any possible way this area could actually somehow have belonged to his ancestors, his parents, and ultimately to him. Unlikely, and yet…

Showy swaths of beach and oat grass were featured in landscaped borders on either side of the storefront. Chunks of beach grass stood in the center of the parking lot in the midst of a poorly landscaped mound. Out of the center of the mound rose a large Carolina pine tree that appeared oddly placed but rose to a stately presence above the rest of the parking lot. Jesper had always thought of the tree and the mound as an oasis in a parking lot desert. The awkward placement was something Jesper had heard Pressley discuss with Mrs. Tara in the past. Past laws made it difficult or impossible to move gravesites when new construction was planned. Consequently, sometimes decisions were made to build around a single or small grouping of old headstones. The small grave sites were simply hidden or incorporated into the planned landscaping, with mixed results. This was the case with The Beach Reed. There had been many objections from the community to the building of the store in the first place, and there had been a legal fight.

Douglas and Dorothy Dyer had headed up an organized group that championed the campaign against the building of The Beach Reed store on the Castinoffs' selected spot. The Dyers and others in the community felt strongly that the remaining worn headstones, though illegible, marked important graves of unknowns who first settled the area. The group considered the area sacred ground and felt it was highly disrespectful to disturb these long-term resting grounds. Although the identities of those buried on the site were not fully established, the Historical Society was continuing efforts to identify those buried there.

Mitch and Tara Castinoff ultimately prevailed in their legal battle, and they built the store about the time that Jesper had begun living alone. The compromise with the Historical Society had been to preserve the headstones within the landscaped area in the middle of the parking lot.

Beach grass, also called marram grass or sand reed, is a genus of two species of sand-binding plants in the grass family. American beach grass grows along the Atlantic coast. European beach grass has been introduced in many places as a dune stabilizer. Native beach grass is protected by law in some areas, and it was protected here.

Jesper always got a chuckle out of Pressley's insistence on referring to the popular decorative Pampus grass as "*pompous*" grass. He tried to explain that the word *pompous* means irritatingly self-important and has nothing whatsoever to do with grass, but the explanation never seemed to stick, so he just helped her plant a bit of "self-important" grass whenever she asked. She never seemed to acknowledge why he jokingly called it her "self-important" grass, and she continued referring to it as *pompous*. Pampus grass did need to be cut back annually, but it provided year-round beauty and interest throughout the area. Many used the grass in dried arrangements, and that was certainly the case at The Beach Reed.

The Beach Reed shop was about a mile from Blondie's and sold multiple items made of grass or reeds (mostly inland grasses and straw rather than the beach grasses that held the dunes of sand together). Hats, baskets, woven jewelry, and the like lined the shelves. The Beach Reed met tourists' needs for beach shirts, shorts, hoodies, swimsuits, mugs, and shell jewelry. In actuality, the owners ordered quite a bit of the merchandise from Amazon, but that did not lessen the beach's ambiance of a sandy, hot day's whimsical purchase.

The Beach Reed was owned by Tara and Mitch Castinoff, who also owned Cooler Beach Realty, a smaller real estate company in the county. Managing The Beach Reed store was Tara's primary source of fun while managing the realty business had become very tedious for her. Mitch managed the business side of real estate, while Tara managed the sales aspects. She felt as though she were in quicksand, dealing with buyers who often had higher expectations than their bank accounts could accommodate. Most of her clients were looking for the same things, and she was tired of hearing their stories and trying to meet their needs.

The Castinoffs were no fan of either Pressley or Jesper. They considered Pressley an island antique whose property should be updated to better uphold the community's standards. They considered Jesper an overly visible and annoying goof whose property should be confiscated. When they or their agents were showing properties, Jesper could often be seen pedaling by on the weathered purple bike. Tara recognized that his visible enjoyment of life helped draw others into the beach atmosphere, and so she was generally friendly toward him during their rare meetings. Jesper seemed to her to be as much a fixture of the community as JW.

Pressley browsed through the selection of straw hats and settled on one with a brightly colored hat band. Tara was behind the counter, looking intently through paperwork, while a dark-skinned young lady with green, spiked hair was waiting to ring up the purchase. Tara looked up and briefly greeted both Jesper and Pressley with, "Oh, hello there." She immediately returned to her activity. Tara's face told stories for those who knew how to read faces. Her eyes seemed deeply set, and they projected a weary sadness for those who engaged her long enough to notice. Her hair was a common brown but sometimes contained lighter tones and highlights added by Blondie. Pressley spoke smilingly. "Good day, Tara. We have a matter to review with you and your husband. Would you happen to have any time later today?"

Tara was clearly irritated. This lady *knew* her husband was an attorney and kept a rather busy schedule, and here she was—playing dumb and wasting Tara's precious time! "Ms. Pressley, you know my husband is an attorney, and I don't manage his schedule. Why don't you call his office and make an appointment?" Tara said impatiently, barely looking up from her paperwork.

The young lady began to ring up the hat purchase while Jesper quickly and sheepishly tossed a new pair of sunglasses in with Pressley's purchase.

"Of course, of course. Sorry, I needed a new sun hat and naturally wanted to buy it from you." Pressley smiled innocently, nodding slightly.

"Well," she responded slowly while beginning to step back, "we think it's likely something to do with this store, actually, and I should have thought to just call Mitch in the first place."

Tara gently and slowly laid the paperwork on the counter and met Pressley's eyes. "Well, if it has to do with the store," she said, her head slowly cocked to the side and her face softening as she looked at both of them as if she were deciding what to say next.

Jesper thought he detected a change in Tara's mood when Pressley mentioned the store. "No, no, dear. Don't you worry," Pressley said, trailing off as she took the bag with the hat and sunglasses from the young lady. She turned and did not look back at Tara while adding brusquely. "We will follow your good advice and call for an appointment."

Tara seemed slightly anxious as she leaned forward to encourage Pressley to go ahead and talk, but Pressley and Jesper were already at the door.

As they entered Pressley's vehicle, Jesper said, "So what do you think?" Jesper tried to see Tara through the storefront windows, but he could only see the person who waited on them appearing to rearrange items behind her. Tara was no longer visible.

"What is *your* opinion?" Pressley smiled as she put the vehicle in reverse, turned back toward the small business area of town, and began to drive.

"Well, she seemed to regret not talking to you. That's what I think," Jesper said.

"And why do you think that is?" Pressley asked.

"It was when you said it had to do with the store. That's when she seemed really interested," Jesper said.

"Good observation," Pressley commented. "And where shall we go next?"

Jesper grinned. "Okay, it's to the lawyer we go."

It was a short drive to Mitch Castinoff's office, which sat just beside the library. Jesper moved to lift the car door handle when

Pressley raised her hand in objection. "No, no. Just wait. It shouldn't take long," she said.

He sat confused momentarily when Tara's car pulled into a parking space at the courthouse, which was across the street from her husband's office. She bolted across the street and straight into the front office door. She did not appear to notice them.

Pressley smiled again, slyly. "Coincidence? I think not. But *now* it is time for us to go in!" Pressley and Jesper both disembarked and made the direct, short walk to the office. When they opened the white door, it brushed past an old-fashioned bell over the doorway that tinkled the announcement of their arrival.

No one was in the waiting room, but a voice from an adjacent room on the left could be heard: "Can I help you?" A middle-aged woman whose voice conveyed a slight air of impatience and irritation appeared. She had on too much lipstick that seemed to be trying to move away from her lips. She peered impatiently over expensive glasses that were secured around her neck with a faux diamond lanyard.

Pressley spoke up quickly. "We wanted to make an appointment to see Mr. Castinoff."

"May I ask what this is about?" asked the woman, removing her glasses and eyeing them both up and down as if she had a built-in scanner.

"Yes, it's about his wife's business, The Beach Reed." Pressley smiled as she raised her voice a bit louder.

Without hesitation, the woman said, "Oh, Mr. Castinoff isn't in today, so I will be glad to take a message."

"Well, we will just talk with his wife if she has time then," Pressley said calmly but with even more purposeful volume.

"She's not here either," insisted the woman.

"I do hate to be pushy," said Pressley somewhat drolly. "However, we just saw Tara come in the door a few moments ago." Pressley paused for effect, and Jesper thought he would melt into the floor, afraid of what she would say next. "Has she left through a back entrance?" Pressley asked while maintaining a sweet smile and scanning the entrance to the hallway where offices were located.

The woman's face and neck immediately flushed bright red. "Let me check. May I have your names?"

Pressley provided their names, and the woman quickly disappeared. They both sat down while waiting. Jesper felt a little uncomfortable, and Pressley could see that he was squirming. "They will see us. Just be patient." It was times like these that left Jesper keenly aware of the differences in their personalities. Wasn't this rude behavior? His thoughts were hovering about what manners really mean, what is polite, and what is not when he heard a male voice coming down a hallway toward them.

Mitch Castinoff appeared, doing his best to smile congenially but clearly anxious and fidgeting painfully while approaching them. "Hello, there! Nice to see you. What can I do for you?" The greeting receptionist had not returned to her post and had disappeared into one of the hallways' closed doors.

"I'll be direct, Mitch," said Pressley, standing and smiling innocently. "We've located the title deed to the property that The Beach Reed sits on. Jesper has copies, and we want to discuss how to best move forward."

Jesper felt the blood drain from his entire body, and he felt frozen. *Was there nothing too embarrassing for Pressley to say?*

"I don't understand. Pardon? What deed are you referring to?" Mitch responded.

"Here is a copy for you," Pressley said, as she took a piece of paper from a small folder she was carrying and offered it to Mitch. She was tempted to say, "*Oh, I am sure you already have copies too!*" but she did not say so. She met Mitch's stern gaze purposefully and waited for him to respond, allowing him to break eye contact first.

Jesper clearly detected Mitch catching his breath and now watched the blood visibly draining from Mitch's face instead of his own.

"Well, I am obviously going to need some time to investigate this. This seems quite confusing," he said, without raising his eyes from the paper but scratching his eyebrow as if terribly puzzled.

"Surely, surely." Pressley smiled sweetly, beaming at Mitch as if she had just won the lottery.

"You have until a week from Monday. Talk to you then, if not before," Pressley said curtly as she headed for the door with Jess closely in tow.

Mitch's face fell in rhythm with each step she took out the door. His attempt at smiling was completely gone once she closed the door.

*****

Pressley had asked Jesper to come by and move the box with her antique finding into her shed. She was away attending tonight's Historical Society meeting. Pressley had not joined the group and didn't have much direct involvement with the Historical Society, but she determined lately that it was time to become involved. Mr. Dyer initiated the society and was currently its acting director. She derisively referred to the group as the "hysterical society" in private conversation, and she wasn't inclined to endorse some of their plans, at least as she understood them. She was in agreement with the society's stated goal of preserving and restoring while also being wary of the motives of some members.

It was dusk when Jess arrived at her home. He laid his bike to the side and bent down to pick up the box that had been left beside her shed. The chickens had gone into their coop, and now one looked out the still-open coop door as if to report back to her poultry colleagues who were milling about. The box was surprisingly heavy. He realized he had not asked her exactly what the box contained, and the box was not sealed. He could not resist looking inside. He saw an odd-looking small metal machine with what appeared to be an arm, which only piqued his curiosity. As soon as he set the box on the work bench in the shed, he removed the machine from the box and set it up on a worktable. He looked around the device and saw that the arm seemed to be for pressing down on a base. He saw a few bits of blank, flat, round metal in the bottom of the box, and he couldn't resist placing one of the disks directly under the arm and pushing it down. When he lifted the arm, he looked down at the result, which was now faintly embossed with the number "12."

He stood dumbfounded. "So it was *Pressley* who gave me the key?" He scratched his head slowly and stood, pondering. "Or the *Dyers*?" This didn't really make sense. He took the key out of his waist pack and compared the two. It seemed clear to him that his key was likely embossed on this machine. Where else had he seen similar embossing? Oh yes, it was on *Anti's collar!*

Jesper closed up the shed slowly while thinking. He could call Pressley, but there was no way she would answer her cell phone. Could she somehow be trying to sabotage his possible ownership of island land? He pedaled slowly home, wondering how these events of the last few weeks fit together. Tomorrow was Saturday, and the church held a fourth Saturday brunch that Pressley and the Dyers helped sponsor. Tomorrow morning, he would find some answers.

CHAPTER 7

The Church

The local church building exterior was primarily made of stone that had been brought in specifically for this building almost a century ago. There were little local rocks and certainly no boulders or large rock occurring naturally around the area, so the building was unique and stood out among the more modern architecture.

Every Sunday at noon, the deep, rich tones coming from church bells could be heard all over the island. Their sound was reminiscent of an English village, the origin of the ancestors who populated these coastal areas in previous centuries. Pressley loved hearing the noon bells, as did almost all of the island's residents. There were no actual bell ringers, but the electronically recorded sounds that reverberated from the building loudspeaker were just as melodic.

The community's most elderly residents all gathered at the church for social events throughout the week. Several of them worked weekly to keep the small, stone-built church building clean and neat. They would mumble and nod in agreement whenever the topic of Jesper's parents came up. *"Yes, they were fine people. They wouldn't have left that boy on his own for the world."*

Attendance at the church was sporadic, and their established minister had moved away several years ago. Some of the men took turns speaking, as they had not made a formal search for a new minister. Much of the time, they simply had informal Bible studies and discussions. J. W. Harriss was not a regular attendee, but he had been sighted during holidays, especially Easter and Christmas. Church wasn't Mr. Harriss's favorite place to visit—way too many women!

Two four-foot rosemary bushes garnished either side of the church's weathered wooden front doors. When it was allowed to grow into a healthy shrub, the rosemary produced tiny blue or white flowers that the bees adored. Every self-respecting islander cooked with fresh rosemary. The plant was used liberally as a culinary herb because of its ready availability, and the growing conditions on the island suited the plant perfectly. On either side of the humble building were two antique stained glass windows, which were the pride of the local members. One of the brightly colored windows showed the Virgin Mary and the angel Gabriel, while the other showed Jesus and Peter at the seashore. Outside, white seagulls scattered along the parking lot and around the grounds, looking for crumbs.

Inside, the building needed an overhaul. There were six long wooden pews on either side of the aisle and a small oak table in front of the speaker's podium that had a carved inset that read "in remembrance of me." The table held the communion supplies. Many coats of white paint had been applied to the few visible doors. The worn hardwood floors were clearly original and gave the building a historical air of an era past.

The church kept a ready supply of freshly harvested honey so they could provide jars to visitors. Admittedly, they did not have many visitors, but the honey was always given away and stayed in demand. The glass jars were prepared with labels that read "John's Bees, Mark 1:6." This was in reference to John the Baptist eating wild honey, and the name worked perfectly since John Carrington was the primary beekeeper.

Mr. and Mrs. Carrington were in their early eighties and had kept honey beehives in the small church courtyard for many years. The three honeybee hives were surrounded by black wrought iron that separated them from the burial grounds that filled one area on the right side of the building. The bee fencing was obviously more modern and recent than that of the burial grounds, but it was necessary for the safety of both the bees and the people. The hives could be easily seen from the fence, with busy bees moving in and out of the hive entrance, depending on the season's activity. Bees commonly travel up to two miles to forage, and in the church location, they were less than two miles from large tulip poplar trees, overgrown wild blueberry bushes, and many other pollinator-friendly plants.

It was a particular source of pride for the Carringtons to maintain these hives each winter when food for bees could become scarce. It was during the spring when hives were most likely to swarm. Swarming means that the bee boxes are too crowded, and the bees move out of their hive, going off to look for better space. The Carringtons managed to keep their bees happy and rarely lost a hive.

Mr. Carrington was in the process of splitting a hive (a method for providing the bees more room and making two hives from one) when Jesper arrived. Through a small courtyard window, Jesper could see a fully suited Mr. Carrington working carefully to lift and adjust frames with the hive box open. Smoke wafted gently from the bee smoker's shiny silver cone-shaped opening. Generally, with the smoke, he could keep the bees calm while doing the necessary work to better the hive. The smoke was intended to mask any "alarm pheromones" that bees might send, alerting the other bees of potential danger. Some people believe that the smoke made bees feel that their hive was on fire. The bees would then be distracted by the idea of the fire, hurry to gorge themselves with honey before the fire destroyed the hive, and hence pay less attention to the hive intruder. Most area beekeepers did not hold to this "fire" theory.

Jesper heard voices coming from the kitchen area, and he wandered in to see if some brunch might already be available. Two long tables were set with seating for twelve each. Jesper quickly found a place and sat, waiting for whatever might be served. Mr. Carrington came in with his bee hat and veil removed but still wearing his suit. He began to unzip the suit as people placed the full dishes on the table and prepared to eat together.

Jesper looked at Pressley, who seemed to be avoiding his gaze. The small crowd took seats, with Mrs. Dyer and Mrs. Carrington continuing to shuttle food and drink to the tables. "Pressley," he blurted, "I used your machine and…" he said, seeming a bit at a loss for words.

He noticed that everyone was now looking at the two of them, and no one was saying anything. "What's going on here?" Jesper asked, looking face-to-face.

Mr. Dyer spoke up, his eyes twinkling. "I guess I will start us off. You left a copy of the deed document on the library's copy machine, Jess. Dorothy took the document she found on the copy machine straight back to me, and we called Pressley."

Jesper felt a little sheepish, remembering that he had gotten distracted by the map on the library wall and, indeed, must have left the second copy on the copy machine.

Mr. Carrington continued, "I have a brother who has practiced law in the capital city for almost forty years. He is close friends with the clerk of court, who helped him research your deed. Once we heard back from them, we knew that the document would stand and that the Castinoffs would have to deal with you, my boy."

Pressley, the Dyers, and the Carringtons all laughed, but Jesper wasn't certain what his mood was. He sat in silent confusion and tried to sort out what was being said.

"What we discovered is that your parents had made the land purchase just days before their accident." Dorothy Dyer spoke up. "Although we still have details to confirm, it's becoming clear that the Castinoffs either knew or should have known that land was *yours*, not theirs! Just before their accident, Mitch was the attorney of record who was to research the property title and ensure there were no liens against the property that your parents purchased. We think that allowed Mitch to be in a position to understand that unless you knew about the land purchase, he and Tara could easily transfer the deed to themselves. Even if you had known, we feel certain that he had a plan to secure the property right out from under you."

Jesper could hardly believe what he was hearing.

"*You own the land that shop sits on*, and they are going to have to come to terms with that!" squealed Mrs. Carrington. She was clearly delighted at the prospect of anyone having any power or influence over the Castinoffs.

"We aren't to revel in the misfortunes of others now, dear," said Mr. Carrington while shaking his head side to side and looking at Mrs. Carrington. He began to pass biscuits and bacon, but no one was paying much attention to the food.

"Well, in Tara's case, I need to make an exception!" said Mrs. Carrington while clapping her hands together. This response elicited amusement from the small group. "Sit! Sit, everyone. We have some brunch to celebrate Jesper's good fortune."

Jesper sat confused, trying to think. "But who put the deed into that box? And the key…and…," he wondered aloud.

Mrs. Dyer smiled slyly. "We thought it might be worth having some fun with. Life is a bit boring now and then, don't you think? We had all but forgotten the old PO boxes, but when we took time to open the ones we could with the few keys taped to the boxes, well, we found what you found." A few were eating slowly now, but everyone was looking at Jesper.

"I was making a new collar for Anti with the antique embossing machine, and as it happened, Pressley came in to talk about how we could possibly help with the deed that had been uncovered. We've had the metal boxes for so many years that I really can't remember how we got them! Probably due to JW's negligence," she said, giggling. "We were trying out the machine to make a new collar for sweet little Anti, when… Well, we just cooked up a fun scheme. And of course, Pressley just had to have that antique embossing machine as a souvenir for the future!" Before he could ask, Mrs. Dyer continued. "Oh, and Douglas. Douglas jogs every day you know. He passes every mailbox on the island if you catch my drift," she said with a wink and smile.

Pressley watched Jesper begin to process these recent events. "Don't be angry with us, dear," she said. "We knew you would enjoy a little mystery, and we needed to give ourselves time to ensure the deed was properly validated before giving the Castinoffs time to counter or scheme further."

"Do you think they will try to fight me for ownership? Actually, I don't want to own a store!" Jesper said, realizing his own thoughts and expressing them out loud.

"Plenty of time to think about that, son," said Douglas Dyer. "The Castinoffs' law firm had also been the firm responsible for managing the holdings of your parents, as you know. As best we can determine, an elderly judge in charge of the case approved their plans, but then he died just two days later. We believe at this point the Castinoffs decided to take advantage of the situation and literally steal your birthright out from under you."

Everyone sat silently for a moment. Mr. Carrington broke the silence and insisted on saying grace before they went any further with the meal. Jesper had already shoved in two bites when he realized he was alone and gulped the last bit slowly as the prayer ended. After Mr. Carrington's prayer for the food, Jesper said haltingly to Pressley, "So when we went to the store to talk to Tara, you already knew the deed was valid?"

Pressley smiled. "Of course. Why else would I proceed in that manner? Remember, all behavior has meaning, and *never ask a question you don't already know the answer to!*"

Jesper thought that *not asking questions you didn't already know the answer to* was a ridiculous thing to say, but he offered no objection and continued to eat more rapidly than the others. Well-browned broccoli and cheddar Quiche, bacon and jelly biscuits, sausage balls, and large slices of beefy red tomatoes—he had filled his plate with everything in reach and was scanning to make sure he hadn't missed some other tasty morsel. He consciously tried to slow his eating down to better mirror his tablemates, but he quickly gave up that endeavor and filled his plate for a second time.

"One of the first things we need to do is find an attorney for you," said Mrs. Carrington as she was carrying dishes back and forth from the kitchen. In unison, Mr. Dyer and Pressley locked eyes and said, "Not Mitch!"

Pressley piped up, "Well, we need to get the appointment before the deadline I gave Mr. Mitch, and that is only a week. I assume your son could help us?" she said, directing this to the Carringtons.

"Wait!" Jesper lowered his fork. "Why did the key fit into that lock at the post office even if it didn't open the box?" he pondered aloud.

"Ah!" said Mr. Dyer. "We knew that the key would open the box here in our shop, and we also knew we could let the deed stay there for safekeeping temporarily. Our best guess is that dear old JW didn't do a thorough job of ensuring proper rekeying of the newer PO boxes. That part still seems like a bit of a mystery, so we decided not to explore it further. After all, JW needs his job as much as anyone on the island."

Heads nodded, and partial agreements were muttered as the food continued to disappear. "Of course, we knew the key did fit the box in our shop, and frankly, we didn't expect you to find the deed so quickly, but you did. You foiled the rest of our little plan, but we can explain that another day."

After most of the meal had been eaten, Pressley spoke up. "So you say you don't want to own The Beach Reed, is that what I heard you say?"

Jesper put down the fork for the final time for this meal. "No way. I just can't see myself owning or running something like that."

Mrs. Carrington was serving coffee to all, and of course, she gave extra to Jesper. "Well, there are a lot of possibilities, including having someone work for you and run it or selling it and having the money to do what you want to!" exclaimed Mr. Carrington as he grinned and leaned forward on the table.

Jesper thought briefly of the small burial ground on the plot of land that he might now be the legal owner of. Could it possibly contain his own ancestors? His parents were buried here, next to the small church building in the center of the community that had grown around it. He was certain of that because he remembered every detail of their funeral. He was still thinking of his parents' funeral when he realized he was home.

Mr. Dyer made an appointment for Pressley and Jesper to meet with the attorney in Raleigh the following week. Jesper was anxious for answers and anxious to proceed with whatever was next. He was full of questions but uncertain how or who to ask! The next couple of days were a blur.

CHAPTER 8

Attorney Time

Jesper Hawthorne earned his first salary as a teenager from a local radio station that had since gone out of business. His parents had left him some money, and because he found little he needed to buy, Jesper had not found it necessary to work at a "regular" job since his parents' death. Jesper enjoyed thinking about the process. After all, a good process is key to good outcomes. Processes can provide certainty and clarity but still allow for change when necessity dictates.

Today, necessity dictated.

Jess, as friends tended to call him, was waiting with Ms. Pressley and Mr. Douglas Dyer in an office in the capital city to meet with an attorney about Jess's potential claim to some property. A deed had been recently discovered that raised the possibility that he might own a valuable piece of property. That particular property was currently owned by attorney Mitch Castinoff and his wife, Tara.

Jesper fidgeted and squirmed in the seat. He felt uncomfortable in the tennis shoes, jeans, and long-sleeved shirt that Ms. Pressley had insisted he wear. He usually wore only shorts, T-shirts, and flip-flops, regardless of the weather. The weather cooperated with Jess's attire because he lived on a coastal inlet that boasted comfortable temperatures most of the year.

This office was nothing like Mitch Castinoff's office. There was a visible assistant who politely greeted and directed steadily-paced visitors. The next difference that Jess noticed was the formality of the many framed degrees displayed on the walls; they seemed to suggest an army of attorneys was bustling behind the modern glass and mahogany maze. Jess had just begun to settle into thought when he realized that Mr. Dyer was loudly greeting his attorney friend and shaking his arm from its socket, one hand on the elbow and the other gripping the attorney's hand. "This is Jesper Hawthorne, the young man we told you about," said Mr. Dyer while gesturing toward Jess to follow his lead.

Those of Jess's generation were less eager to shake hands for several reasons, but given that he was not with those of his generation at the moment, Jess took a deep breath and slowly put forward his outstretched hand. The attorney, Maxwell Carrington, smiled and politely returned the greeting with a light handshake while inviting the three to an office room down a hallway. Once everyone was seated, coffee and water were served. Pressley sat erect with perfect posture, topped by her small, gray-haired bun looking a bit like a cherry on a cupcake. She directed a purposeful stare across the large table directly at Jess. He became aware that the purpose of her stare was likely to raise his awareness that using six sugars and three creamers was not acceptable in such a public setting. After the third sugar packet, Jess became fully aware of her unspoken guidance, and he stopped adding to his coffee and tried to turn his attention to those in the room.

Maxwell Carrington was a stocky, well-dressed man in his midfifties, with closely cropped, graying hair. He had an open laptop and several documents arranged neatly on the table in front of him. He smiled broadly toward Jesper and said with a booming, distinct Carolinian drawl, "I understand you, sir, are the owner of The Beach Reed. Congratulations on your newest acquisition!"

Jess wasn't sure how to respond, but he relaxed as Mr. Dyer and Pressley both chuckled aloud simultaneously.

"Now, Maxwell," said Mr. Dyer. "The boy needs some clarity and answers to questions about this whole matter. Let's hear your recommendation on what his options are."

The meeting seemed like a blur to Jess, who was not enjoying being away from the island, as the locals called it.

Jesper did not take offense to being frequently referred to as a *boy* by some of his older friends. He was comfortable in his own home and found little need to travel away from the immediate community where he lived. Jesper was prone to panic attacks and didn't see any reason to put himself in unfamiliar situations. He had not shared with Pressley his concern that dealing with a place like The Beach Reed might trigger his panic attacks. Since he learned that he may be the legal owner of the place, he had actually avoided biking or walking past that very familiar part of the island.

Mr. Carrington looked down at the paperwork in front of him and bit his lip repeatedly while looking back and forth between the papers and the three of them.

"Son, I think you take these two sleazebags right to court. That's what I'd do," he said, looking at his paperwork and plopping it on the table. "Course, we can write them a 'come-to-Jesus' letter first and start that way. A subpoena or the letter—you tell me what you want to do." With a firm slap of his hand down on the desk, Maxwell Carrington leaned back as if to communicate that his contribution was finished for today.

A discussion ensued, with Jess not sure what to say. Pressley and Mr. Dyer asked several questions while continuing to try, unsuccessfully, to defer to Jesper and engage him in the dialogue.

"Jesper mentioned to me last week at the church brunch that he didn't really want to own a place like The Beach Reed, didn't you, Jess?" Pressley said calmly and slowly.

This question made Jess focus, and he nodded his head and felt his face go red. He just didn't know how to respond, despite the last few sleepless nights he had spent thinking about the situation.

"Well, there is plenty of time to figure out whether you're a store proprietor or a rich beach bum. We just need to get the court involved one way or another. Let's start with the letter, okay? I can send it to you by email, and ya'll just let me know it's okay, and we'll get this ball rollin'," Mr. Carrington said brusquely, clearly in a hurry to move on to his next client.

The meeting seemed to pass oddly like a blur as the trio were heading back to the island. Pressley drove her Land Rover 90 with

Mr. Dyer in the front seat and Jess sitting in the rear, side-facing seat. Jess watched in silence as they passed pines and palms with telephone lines sparsely interspersed between. "A rich beach bum"—this phrase stuck in Jess's mind. *I am not a bum, and I doubt that one property would make me* rich, he thought. It occurred to him at that point that he had not even asked about potential value! He had been so caught up in the fear of being faced with new people, new conflicts, and new unknowns.

Mr. Dyer turned in his seat and handed a folder back to Jesper. "Here is your copy of everything to date, Jess," he said. "Have you looked up the tax value of your future property?"

"No, no, I haven't," Jess quickly replied. He was amazed by his own words as he realized that he had not. Pressley was glancing in the rearview mirror, darting her eyes between the road and Jess.

"Well, we have," said Mr. Dyer, grinning.

"And?" said Jess. His phone was in his hand even now, and he had plenty of time to research the value of the property, yet he had not.

"How does five million sound to you?" Mr. Dyer grinned.

Jess didn't respond immediately as they pulled to the side of the small, gravelly, paved road in front of Jess's house.

Although Jess's property had never been severely damaged by a hurricane or flooding despite its close proximity to the ocean, the salt air and high humidity had taken their toll. His father had been a handyman operating a small "jack of all trades" local carpentry business, and Jess had learned much from accompanying him. Jess had done his best to replace rusty hinges and repaint and keep his small blue stucco beach home land-worthy.

Jesper opened the front door and invited Mr. Dyer and Ms. Pressley inside. Both gingerly stepped inside, past the bike helmet hanging on the porch, and made their way through the cluttered front room to the small kitchen table. Jess laid his folder down on the table. His hands both rested on his front-facing fanny pack. "So the value of the property that The Beach Reed sits on would bring *five million dollars?*" Jess asked as his eyes widened a bit.

"Probably so, probably so! We think at least that much." Pressley smiled.

Jess's mind went back to the somewhat disguised grave site that sat in the middle of the parking lot on the land that housed The Beach Reed. "The Beach Reed is a spot everyone on the island knows, and tourists are always in there," Jess said aloud. "What if I didn't sell it? Would you want to run it?" he asked, looking up at Pressley.

"Oh, darling boy, I don't think we should get that far ahead of ourselves. Let's see what the Castinoffs have to say once they receive Mr. Carrington's love letter."

Pressley and Mr. Dyer said polite goodbyes and headed out of Jess's home. As he closed the door, he began to worry about how and whether he could avoid Tara and Mitch Castinoff for the upcoming months while all this was being sorted out.

CHAPTER 9

Gondolas

Jesper's cellphone had the maximum number of ringtones by the time he fumbled for it and looked to see who was calling him at sunrise. Actually, it wasn't sunrise, but since he was just awakening, it was sunrise to him. *Why would anyone be calling this early?* he thought. The incoming call displayed as an *unknown caller*, but based on the area code, it was clearly a local number. Jess's mind immediately went to the fact that Mitch and Tara Castinoff would likely respond quickly to the attorney's formal notification of Jess's legal claim.

His online search confirmed that the number indeed belonged to Mitch Castinoff.

He wasn't about to return the call, but on the other hand, he didn't feel right about asking Pressley to do so. No voice message—thank goodness—meant he didn't have to respond immediately. After coffee and a pop-tart breakfast, he pondered at the kitchen table what he should do next. Jess left a few dirty dishes from yesterday piled in the sink and headed out on his trusty bike.

He passed the homes of neighbors—some he knew and some he did not. Many rented their homes out, so it was difficult to know those neighbors because different people were always coming and going. He felt the buzz of his phone and pedaled slower so that he could read the incoming text message. The Dyers needed a babysitter for Anti, and this text was asking if she could stay with him for the week they were gone. He enjoyed Anti's visits and had thought that the next time she visited, he would add a basket to his bike and teach her to ride in it. He pulled to the side of the road and began to respond to Mr. Dyer with a short text. He was lost in drafting his response when he heard a car door open behind him and looked up.

Mitch Castinoff was standing in front of his bike, hands on hips, and a nasty scowl on his face. "Why, you little *punk-ass*! You stupid little insignificant *snot*. That's what you are. If you think you and any of these *stupid* small-town yokels are going to take our business, you have another thing coming." Jesper thought at any moment that steam might literally be coming out of Mr. Castinoff's ears.

"You think you're a big man now, don't you?" Mitch continued without taking a breath. You don't look like such a big man without your grandmother to hide behind, you putz."

At the mention of Pressley as his "grandmother," Jess began to feel irritated.

Mitch continued, "Let me tell you something…"

While he was trying to figure out how or if he should respond to such an angry man, he noticed out of the corner of his eye that Tara Castinoff was in the passenger seat of the gray Mercedes they were driving.

Tara's gaze was downward, and she did not look up while Mitch continued his increasingly loud tirade. Jess became aware of two passing cars that did not pay them any notice.

"And I can promise you, you *will* regret this, you…you stupid, little, arrogant jerk, by God!" Mitch growled through gritted teeth while storming back into his car and slamming the door. He left a dust cloud settling on Jess as his tires spun furiously on the partial gravel pavement. Jess waited until the dust had lessened, and then he took a deep breath and collected his thoughts. One good thing was that the initial confrontation he had been dreading was now in the past. A second positive was that it seemed certain that Mitch must have received the legal notice.

Jess remained stopped, straddling his bike, and noticed his surroundings much more clearly than he had before being the subject of Mitch's angry tirade. A feeling of sadness and dread began to envelop him. The sun was rising in a clear crimson blue sky, and Jess could hear the faint sounds of the ocean lapping at the shore in the distance, occasionally interrupted by the screeching of seagulls. He began to think about why turmoil seemed so ever present with people. Surrounding nature reflected peace and tranquility, but that peace seemed elusive when humans were involved. How depressing it was to be around a person like Mitch Castinoff and how quickly his influence had changed Jess's mood for the worse.

A honking car horn startled him so much that he almost jumped off the bike. Mr. Dyer was just pulling in on the side of the road behind him, with Anti panting visibly in the windshield.

"Hi, there, Mr. Hawthorne!" barked Mr. Dyer as he jumped from his car and trotted toward Jesper. "Flat tire or just taking in the scenery?" he asked as he approached Jesper.

Jesper smiled and looked back to see Anti's tail furiously wagging while she appeared to be simultaneously dripping spit onto Mr. Dyer's truck dashboard and rubbing nose smudges against the windshield glass.

"Well, truthfully, I was just going to ride around and think," Jesper said. "Nothing's wrong with the bike."

"Why don't we meet up at Gondola's? It will soon be lunchtime, and it will be my treat. Dorothy would love me to bring in some spaghetti. She's back opening the store, and I was just on my way to…well, just meet me there," said Mr. Dyer, turning away and back to his car before Jess had a chance to agree or disagree. He watched Douglas Dyer and Anti disappear in the distance. Their sudden familiar appearance and rapid movement away made him wonder, *Why was he so dreading the big changes that seemed certain ahead?*

Gondola's Pizza and Spaghetti was a favorite restaurant of his. Jess leaned his bike against the building next to the small restaurant and headed inside. Mr. Dyer had already chosen a seat, and Anti was lying on the floor beside his chair. Like many people in the small town, the owner, Mikos Lainos, loved dogs and allowed them in his establishment. Mikos had opened the restaurant about twenty years prior. His menu was not elaborate, consisting of limited choices of simple Greek American, but his food was so consistently of good quality that his restaurant was busy six days per week from the time the doors were open. Mikos believed in managing the menu to just a small number of foods but doing them perfectly. Mikos was six feet and five inches tall, with bright gray hair and one of the biggest chins that Jess had ever seen. A dish towel was usually over his right shoulder as he made his frequent rounds from table to table to greet and welcome his customers.

Jess took a seat. He didn't notice Mikos in the restaurant today. Only after looking around did Jess notice that The Beach Reed was faintly visible in the distance from where he sat. He cut his gaze away from the store immediately to see Mr. Dyer smiling toward him. "That crook has a deadline of this Monday to respond to Mr. Carrington's letter. What makes you think you couldn't manage the store and the property?" Douglas said, reaching down to pet Anti reassuringly.

"It isn't that I couldn't. I think it's more that I don't *want* to," Jess replied, looking down at the red and white checkered tablecloth.

"What can I get for you, gentlemen?" asked the waitress. "We got a two-slice plus drink and salad special today," she began when Douglas interrupted her.

"Perfect, we will take two of those," he said. "And I need some spaghetti and meatballs to go."

The waitress smiled at Jess, never making eye contact with Mr. Dyer. "How in the world are you? You haven't been in here in the past couple of weeks."

"Yeah, I've been kind of busy," Jess replied.

Mr. Dyer thought he detected some slight redness in Jess's face. "I told you I've been waiting for you to ask me out, and I'm *stilllll* waiting." She leaned in just a little closer to Jess. "But I'll bring your lunch while you decide where we're going!" she said matter-of-factly and proceeded to make her way to the next table.

Mr. Dyer had leaned back in his chair. "I could just ignore that rather than ask questions about her." Mr. Dyer smiled.

"Oh, that's Camelia. She's been after me for a while now." Jess grinned.

Mr. Dyer leaned across the table and lowered his voice. "She's certainly pretty. You could do worse!" he said.

Jess secretly agreed, but he felt those types of matters were private, and he changed the subject back to the impending legal battle. "I want to talk with Pressley again. Maybe she wants to manage the store. She has a lot more experience than I do," Jess said.

Mr. Dyer rested his folded hands on the table, and they sat in silence once Jess had trailed off. After a long silence, Mr. Dyer spoke up. "Why do you want to limit yourself to Pressley?" he asked quietly.

The question struck Jess as intrusive…even as he realized what a strong substitute grandmother or mother figure she had been in his life. "I'm not limiting myself!" he blurted. "It's just that…well, she's familiar, and she's consistent—a known entity, you know? And maybe I shouldn't sell it right away, that is, if I get it. Maybe I should explore it first and consider the possibilities, and the cost-benefit ratio. I mean, I don't even know whether that store runs a profit. Or maybe they fund it from one of their other businesses?"

Mr. Dyer patiently listened to Jess as he worked through his thoughts aloud. Douglas Dyer asked questions, and these questions prompted Jess to think differently than when Jess was alone on his own couch absorbed in his own thoughts. After listening for a good while to Jess working through his thoughts and expressing his feelings, Mr. Dyer spoke. "One thing I do want to offer you as you consider what to do. You have more life experience than you think, Mr. Hawthorne. Do not sell yourself short." He smiled.

They continued their conversation focused on Jess's thoughts about what he would do with the property until their meal arrived. Their pizza was being placed in front of each of them before they realized that Camelia had been close enough to hear their conversation. "Don't know what store you are talkin' 'bout, hon, but sure am good with the customers!" She grinned. "Keep me in mind whatever it is. And I get off at eight tonight. Meet you at the pier right afterward!" she said to Jess as she left them with a full table of salad, drinks, and pizza.

Mr. Dyer remarked without thinking, "That's about how Dorothy and I met…," but he trailed off quickly as he realized that might not be what Jess wanted to hear.

After they finished their meal, they agreed on a date and time for the Dyers to drop off Anti on their way out of town for their upcoming trip to pick up new items for their store. Jess began unzipping his fanny pack to pay for the meal when Mr. Dyer said, "I invited you. Let me pay this time. Enjoy it while you can. Once your ship comes in, I plan to be on that cruise frequently! And I would say I won't be the only one." He laughed and winked.

Eight o'clock that evening found Jess and his bike at the pier.

Jess did love this beach life, but he wasn't a great surfer, and he did not enjoy fishing. His thoughts were on a nearby sea turtle-hatching site that was being guarded by volunteers when Camelia plopped down beside him.

Both of them looked forward. "Told you I'd get you. It might take a while, but I always win," she said matter-of-factly, looking out over the horizon. Camelia and Jess had been in high school together, with Camelia being two years younger than Jess. Camelia had been a witness to Jess's very public panic attack on the day of driver's ed. She had loved Jess since middle school, but somehow he did not feel ready to be "gotten," as she put it.

"So tell me what you and Mr. Dyer were talking about. I'm dying to know!" she asked.

Jess kept his gaze on the horizon, wondering whether Camelia might be just the person to confide in. He had intended to go to Pressley's tonight and talk, but fate seemed to have a different idea.

Once Jess explained the situation to Camelia, she squealed, "Oh boy! Oh boy! But wait, Aunt Tara runs The Beach Reed, and she won't be happy!"

"Tara is your *aunt?*" Jess asked, looking at Camelia with his eyes widening and his mouth hanging open.

"Aunt Tara and Uncle Mitch, yeah. Tara is my mom's sister," Camelia added, seemingly unaware of the significance of what she was saying.

Jess became visibly uncomfortable and turned his gaze back to the horizon.

"My uncle is a bit of a dipshit," she said. "Even Mom and Dad think so. We've never been one of those Hallmark families anyway."

"Cammie, you can't say anything to anyone about this," said Jess, but even as the words were leaving his mouth, he realized that the entire community would become aware, if they weren't already.

"I won't," she said quickly. "I have to close and open the next few days, so I won't have time to think, much less talk to friends." She looked directly at Jess. "But I do have time for *you*."

They sat talking for hours under a majestic mead moon that made the pier and their spirits brighter as the night wore on.

Pressley

Jess found the package with the dog basket that he had ordered from Amazon on his front porch. He excitedly put the basket onto his bike and stood back to look at it, wondering how Anti would look inside it and whether she would be comfortable. He jumped on the bike and headed to Pressley's to show off his new find.

His heart sank, and he felt ill when he saw an ambulance in front of Pressley's home. He skidded to a stop on the bike and threw it to the ground, denting the new dog basket. The door was open, and he went inside slowly as if moving more slowly might prevent him from seeing Pressley hurt or injured. He saw Pressley on a stretcher and heard radio communications coming from the emergency medical technician and from the ambulance.

"Are you family?" asked the EMT, who was not talking on the radio. "No, I'm not, but she doesn't have any close family here," said Jess. His mind raced at the question: Did she have any family at all? Why didn't he know?

"We're taking her to the hospital. You can follow us or ride with us if you want," they said, raising the rails on the stretcher and beginning to wheel it out the front door. Pressley did not seem to be moving or conscious.

"Is she going to be alright?" he asked.

"It's best to let the doctor sort out the diagnosis and prognosis. Just come over to the hospital if you don't want to ride with us."

This was a strong example to Jess of why he should try again to get his driver's license. He was angry at himself for procrastinating about the driver's test. The hospital was a little too far to get there as quickly as he would like on his bike, so he decided to enter the back of the ambulance. He was afraid that if he looked at Pressley's face, he would not get a response, so he kept his gaze down and tried to hold her hand. Her hand did not respond to his touch, and he gently pulled his hand back and started to say a silent prayer.

He began to feel ill and felt a familiar old pain in his chest. Sweating, he looked at the EMT riding in the back and monitoring Pressley's life signs.

"Are you okay?" asked the technician.

This is the last thing that Jess remembered before he woke up in the emergency room.

*****

Jesper looked around the room and tried to focus. Someone was adjusting a dial on a machine he seemed vaguely connected to. He heard another voice in the background saying, "No, we didn't find a driver's license or any other IDs on him."

"Can you tell me your name?" said the person at the bedside, whom he realized must be a nurse. "Jesper Hawthorne," he replied.

"Good. Can you tell me your address?" she asked next.

"102 South Drive," he responded. "And before you ask, it's Thursday, and the month is July."

"Alright." She chuckled. "You pass the test. Can you tell me what the last thing you remember is?"

"Pressley, what about my friend Pressley?" Jess asked.

"She's been admitted," the nurse replied.

Jess relaxed a bit immediately because it seemed that meant Pressley would recover. A young doctor walked in, along with the EMT Jess had been riding with.

"Pretty clever way to get out of walking in here," joked the EMT. "Do you have a history of seizure?"

"No, no, but I do have panic attacks and some other issues I deal with," Jess said. "Did I have a seizure?"

"Not necessarily, but I think it's one of the things that needs to be ruled out. We'll schedule a couple of tests for you, and then we'll get you out of here shortly," finished the doctor. He was scribbling and clicking into a large electronic file pad as he was turning to leave.

Jess gathered himself up on his elbows and called to the doctor, "What about Ms. Pressley, my friend? Is she going to be okay?"

The EMT leaned in. "She's the lady we were bringing in with him."

Jess noticed the EMTs' name badge, and he couldn't make out the last name, but the first name said "Anthony."

"Are you her son, or are you family?" asked the doctor. The doctor's name was plainly visible on his immaculate lab coat: Dr. Dennis Kinsman.

"Well, I'm the closest thing to family that she has, but no, I'm not her son," Jess replied.

"Probably best for you to just visit with her once you are discharged, okay?" the doctor said as he again headed quickly out the door.

The nurse came to discharge Jess and gave him paperwork with instructions for home care and for scheduling two follow-up tests. She handed Jess a plastic bag with his cell phone inside it. It was then that Jess noticed his fanny pack was not on his waist.

"Hey, did my bag get left in the ambulance or something?" Jess asked the nurse. "It was around my waist when I went to Pressley's house."

"I'll check, but we didn't remove anything from you," interrupted the EMT casually.

The nurse responded. "Our process is to put patients' belongings in a bag, especially someone who isn't conscious or responsive. I bet you'll find that you left it at home. If not, call the hospital lost-and-found. Maybe they can help."

Jess felt ill. His hiding place for the original deed document was, of course, his waist belt, which he rarely removed. His mind raced through the past few hours' events, and he was certain he had the pack on when he entered the ambulance. He also remembered carrying his phone inside one of the leather bag's pockets.

*****

Jess went from the emergency room into Pressley's room as if he were entering a funeral home. Pressley appeared asleep, and he didn't want to wake her, so he sat alone at her bedside for about an hour, thinking about what he should do. He pulled out his cell phone and made a call to Maxwell Carrington's office.

He was fortunate to be transferred directly to Mr. Carrington's line and was able to speak to him immediately without leaving a voice message. "I think I have lost the original deed," Jess blurted.

"This isn't going to make our case any easier." Mr. Carrington sighed. "We've already looked up what's in the courthouse records. Our staff is on it like white on rice. Mitch isn't stupid, and he does have connections, you know. I am filin' our case, and he will be notified, and we will go from there. I do have the copy of the deed, of course, but you had the original, and that is a real problem. How is Ms. Pressley? I heard she's in the hospital. Is she going to be okay?" Mr. Carrington asked. He asked in a rapid-fire, impatient manner just as he spoke, with Jess half expecting him to hang up before Jess answered.

"I'm waiting to talk to the doctor now," Jess said. Just then, the door opened slowly, and in walked a nurse and a doctor. Jess ended his call with Maxwell Carrington, promising to update Mr. Carrington on Pressley's condition as soon as possible, and then anxiously turned his attention back to the bedside.

"Is she going to be okay?" he asked.

The doctor smiled and nodded slightly, introducing himself and the nurse by name. Jess didn't retain their names and did not offer his. "We're still running tests and in the process of making a clearer diagnosis," he said. "Was anyone with her when she became ill?"

"No, not to my knowledge," Jess said, turning to look at her. "I was on my way to see her that morning. I guess she felt ill, and then she called 911?" he continued.

"As I understand it, that's a fair assumption, but we don't have much information," said the doctor. He focused carefully on Jess's face. "Is there anyone who might wish her harm?"

This question startled Jess, and he blurted anxiously, "What do you mean? Has someone hurt her?"

"Well, we're clarifying a diagnosis, but she hasn't been awake since we admitted her, and so we have limited information. We have a series of routine questions that one of the nurses will go through with you. I would like to stay in touch with you if there aren't any family members we can communicate with. We also have the names of Mr. and Mrs. Dyer with whom we've spoken. They were here earlier."

The nurse asked Jess a series of questions, trying to elicit anything helpful about Pressley's medical history, but Jess realized he knew little about Ms. Pressley's past, much less her medical history. Had she fallen? Had anyone been with her? What was the last time anyone had seen her? Was she a heavy drinker? He began to think about their relationship and was almost panicked at thinking she might not live. His parents had known her, and she had been the most significant presence in his life since the funeral. She was indeed his primary link to the past. Jess shared all his personal contact information with the hospital and explained that he and Pressley had been friends since his parents died.

CHAPTER 11

Progress

Jess and Camelia met again that night at the pier after her shift ended. Jess again confided in Camelia, telling her all about the day's events. He shared his fear that someone might have hit Pressley over the head, poisoned her, or who knows what.

"Why would anyone want to hurt her? Everyone loves Ms. Pressley," Camelia said. "She's also a great tipper. I love to see her coming into the shop because I know I'll at least have her tip that day!" She smiled at Jess and realized he was too deep in thought to be amused by anything she might say.

"I have a connection that might help us somehow," she said. "Another family member. My cousin, Anthony, is an EMT. He might know something."

"Your *cousin*? You mean related to Mitch and Tara?" he said.

"Sure. Anthony is their son," Cammie said.

Jesper closed his eyes and thought carefully before asking Cammie his next question.

"I want to ask a favor of you, Cammie," Jesper said.

Cammie responded with a strained smile. "Anything."

"It's kind of odd, but here goes. Without letting anyone else know, could you snoop around Anthony and his place to find out if he has my waist pack?" Jesper asked.

"What! I noticed you didn't have it on, and I never see you without it. I started to ask you about it. Maybe you left it at Pressley's?" she asked, glancing downward.

Jess sensed her hesitation. "No way. I had it on when I passed out in the ambulance," Jess responded. After an awkward pause, Jess asked Cammie what her silence meant.

"It's just that Anthony has been in and out of trouble most of his life. If he is stealing again and he gets caught, I don't know what that will mean," Cammie said. "Tell you what. I'll take a look around his apartment tomorrow and meet you at the pier at the same time tomorrow night, okay?"

Jess replied, "I really, really appreciate it. Thank you, Cammie."

Camelia smiled to herself contentedly when she heard Jess refer to her as *Cammie*.

*****

Jess tried different things all day, hoping to distract himself from his constant worry about Pressley and from the anxiety he felt at the loss of his leather waist bag. He found the hours stubbornly dragging until he and Camelia were back on the pier.

Camelia took off a backpack she was wearing and laid it on the pier between them. She took a deep breath, opened the backpack slowly and purposefully, and then removed Jess's leather waist bag, handing it to him.

He began to unzip the pockets to look for the contents he recalled being in the pack as Cammie commented in a disappointed tone, "Yes, it was right there among plenty of other things that I know aren't his."

"My pack's empty! Crap! I had several things in here I really needed, including the original deed to the land." He looked across at Cammie and offered a weak smile. "I really appreciate you getting this back for me."

"Oh, you are welcome. I just don't know what to do next," Cammie replied while focusing her gaze on the weather-beaten wooden pier beneath, ocean waves visibly lapping the sand below.

Jess realized that he had not considered the impact that these recent events had on Cammie.

He reached out to put his hand on her shoulder and said, "I know this wasn't easy for you to do, and I want you to know I really, really appreciate it."

Cammie's head remained lower, and she did not respond to his expression of appreciation.

"So we can't really call the police because Anthony will just deny that he had the bag, and then he may figure out you took it. But whatever he has done with my deed and my credit card and—Oh no. I gotta put a block on that card!" Jess said as he scrambled to stand and urgently dial the credit card company.

"How about an anonymous call to the police? To tip them to check for stolen goods in Anthony's apartment?" Jess said, looking down at the top of Cammie's head.

"That will just kill my aunt Tara," Cammie offered meekly. "But I suppose it's the right thing to do, but I started thinking…"

Jess listened. Cammie suggested that instead of calling the police immediately, Jess first use the new information about Anthony to help motivate Mitch and Tara to back down from their attack on him and their apparently false claim to The Beach Reed land. He wasn't certain about the ethics of this approach, and he wished that Pressley were there to give him some advice. Pressley! He hadn't even visited her today. "Can you go with me to visit Pressley?" Jess asked while waiting on hold with the credit card company.

"Sure, and I can on Thursday too. That's my day off this week," Cammie responded.

"Okay, great. Maybe you want to come for dinner one night this week?" he said, phone to his ear and shuffling his feet while looking between the cracks of the pier boards.

Cammie replied, "Not only will I come over, but I'll get Mikos to make you an extra-large, and I'll bring it with me!" Cammie realized Jess was now completely engrossed in follow-up about his returned bag, putting a hold on the missing credit card, and on Ms. Pressley's condition. "I'm going home tonight, but I'll talk to you tomorrow." She kissed Jess on the cheek and walked back toward her car.

Jess had no sooner placed the phone back into his leather bag than it began vibrating like a buzzer. He answered quickly and found himself talking with a nurse who wanted to provide an update that Ms. Pressley's condition had been upgraded from critical to stable; however, she had not yet regained consciousness and so was not talking. Jess headed home, exhausted and looking forward to sleeping.

The next morning, Jess called Mr. Carrington's office to bring him up to speed on current events. Mr. Carrington listened to Jess's story about how he and Cammie suspected Anthony had removed Jess's fanny pack and may have even given the original land document to Mitch.

"Leave it to me," replied Mr. Carrington, and he hung up without even saying goodbye.

Jess began to wonder whether Mr. Maxwell Carrington was the attorney for him, but before he engaged anyone else, he wanted to allow time for Pressley to recover. Mr. Carrington was certainly not the warm-and-fuzzy listener that Mr. Dyer was, but maybe that was just a characteristic of lawyers. Mr. Carrington was the son of the Carringtons, who had long been friends of Pressley, and he didn't want to do anything that might upset those relationships.

Jess scrolled through his phone, looking to orient himself as much as he was seeking distraction. He initially spent the morning trying to clean his home but abandoned that effort well before lunch. He felt the pull of The Beach Reed and decided no one could object to his riding past on public streets. After he had ridden past twice, he ventured slowly over to the part of the parking lot that contained the old gravestones. This area had not been well maintained, and it occurred to Jess that the Castinoffs must consider the graves not significant or worthy of their time and attention. He was partially hidden in the small areas of underbrush as he looked around. The few stones were weathered bare, with a couple that seemed likely to have had carvings that had given way and were crumbling under the earth's elements, rain, lichen, and black fungus.

Jess had learned a little about landscaping from spending time with Pressley. He looked up at the shape of the pine tree that rose in the middle of the graves and thought that some strategic pruning could greatly improve the look of the site. Perhaps a small fence and clearing the worst of the brush? He wondered what the Historical Society had determined about these graves. His thoughts were interrupted by a car door. Through the brush and hidden from her view behind the trunk of the tree, Jess saw Tara enter the building alone. She appeared to have been crying, but from this distance, he could not see much detail. He had not bothered to see whether the store was open or who might be inside. Jess thought it best to keep a low profile until he officially gained ownership, if that ever occurred. Meeting Mitch Castinoff again in any setting was the last thing he wanted. Another car arrived, and the occupant did not seem to notice Jess's bike near the grave area. The man went inside the store, and then a couple more cars arrived with a few people who appeared to be headed for a day of fun at the beach.

Jess looked down at the gravestones again and decided he would begin to attend the Historical Society meeting and start the process of finding out whether any of these sites contained his ancestors' remains.

A REGULAR CURIOSITY

Jess reached for his ringing cellphone. He recognized Mr. Carrington's number. "Hello?" he answered.

In his usual cryptic, brief communication style, Mr. Maxwell Carrington said, "Meeting. We'll have a meeting at my office. It's an important one. Can you be there tomorrow at 3:00 p.m.?"

"Yes, I'll be there," Jess said. He immediately called the Dyers to confirm that one of them would be able to drive him the couple of hours it would take to reach Mr. Carrington's office. Mr. and Mrs. Dyer agreed that Dorothy would watch the store, and Douglas would be available to drive Jess to the attorney's office for the meeting. Douglas and Jess agreed to check on Pressley at the hospital before heading over to Mr. Carrington's office.

Mr. Dyer asked Jess what the meeting was about, and Jess replied, "Truthfully, I forgot to ask! He really didn't give me time to ask. He just said we should come to a meeting and that it was important."

*****

As they walked into Mr. Carrington's office, they were surprised to see Tara Castinoff sitting at the far side of the table. Her head was lowered, and she made no eye contact with either of them. She had clearly been crying. Mr. Carrington seated them quickly and began to talk rapidly in his strong Carolina accent.

"We'll just get right to it. Ms. Tara is here to sign over the property to you, Mr. Hawthorne," said Maxwell Carrington. He threw his head back while offering his next communication, and Jess became

65

focused on Mr. Carrington's eye tics and rapid blinking, something he had not noticed before in their first meeting. "Once we complete signings today and get everything registered, that will be the end of the Castinoffs' legal claim to the property. Because The Beach Reed sits on your property, it is agreed in these documents that you become the sole owner of it and everything that sits on the said property."

Mr. Dyer and Jess were stunned. Mr. Dyer spoke up first. "You mean the meeting today is to sign over the property and the store completely—lock, stock, and barrel—to Jesper Hawthorne?"

Mr. Carrington adjusted his tie while wiggling his neck within a shirt collar that was clearly too tight and said, "That's it exactly."

Tara's body language reflected depression and defeat. Jess almost began to feel very sorry for Tara. "I just want to say…well…" Tara stammered. After a heavy sigh and deep breath, she said, "I want to say I'm sorry. I'm just sorry for the way things turned out. We really didn't start out doing anything wrong. We really, really didn't. We were struggling, and Anthony had to be bailed out again and…" She started to cry.

Jess listened, but he did not respond. Jess began to feel overwhelmed, and he felt a pain starting in his chest. He mentally turned his attention to breathing more slowly and deeply as he started to worry that he would have a panic attack. This just wasn't the place for another attack! Maybe the therapy that Pressley had been insisting on wasn't such a bad idea. He had resisted that idea for years, despite urging from his doctor and from Pressley. The room seemed to be getting smaller, and he reached for a glass of water and struggled to turn his attention back to what Tara was saying. He began to try to breathe deeply and slowly while paying enough attention and concentrating on Tara's words. He just heard mumblings while trying to gain internal control over his anxiety. It all sounded rambling and raised more questions for him than it answered. He began to process again and hear what she was saying.

"And the community needed a store for tourists, at least that's what we told ourselves. Your father had a hand in getting Anthony arrested, and…I really thought at the time that we were saving our son and helping the community. I realize we took something from you, but it was something you never had, so…" Tara began to cry even more so much so that she could not talk.

Maxwell Carrington looked at Jess and raised his eyebrows slightly. "I did say Mitch had connections, but I have some too. My staff will be in here with paperwork for ya'll to sign. Hate to bring this up." He pointed an index finger at Jess. "You'll get my bill, but you can afford me," he said while adding a large grin as he left the room.

Jess looked across at Tara, who was blowing her nose and still looking down at the table. "Will you be okay?" he asked as she began dabbing her eyes with a Kleenex.

"Yes, yes. Thanks for asking. I'll be fine. We're probably going to be getting a divorce, but one way or another, I will be okay," she responded.

Thoughts and questions were flooding into Jess's mind. The one he chose to ask was, "Doesn't Mitch need to be here with you for the signing?"

Mr. Carrington leaned forward eagerly as if to "second" the question.

"No, he doesn't. It's my name on the deed," she answered.

Jess thought carefully before asking his question. "Could you possibly keep running The Beach Reed for the next few weeks or months while I figure things out?" Jess asked slowly and deliberately.

This question sent her into sobs of crying, and Jess began to feel even more sympathy for her. She was nodding her head *yes* while crying, so Jess felt relieved that he didn't have to make any quick decisions about the property under these circumstances. He had never seen her in any situation where she wasn't exuding complete, controlled confidence, and this was quite unsettling.

Mr. Dyer felt as if he were watching a movie and as if he were having an out-of-body experience. He excused himself during the signings and called his wife to let her know of this unexpected turn of events. She shared the good news that Pressley was now awake and conversing with her just within the past hour. Douglas Dyer was able to relay this good news to Jess as they left the attorney's office and began to make their way back to the island.

As they came back into the community, Mr. Dyer drove slowly past The Beach Reed. The store and the property appeared completely different to Jess than any of the hundreds, if not thousands, of times that he had passed by them before. They drove straight to the hospital and fortuitously arrived just before the end of the published visiting hours.

Jesper thought to himself that, despite his familiarity with her, Pressley appeared as different to him as the store had. Both were so familiar, but now they seemed completely new and unfamiliar. She was awake as he approached her bedside, and she turned her head toward him. "So I understand things are working out well for you, my little friend!" she said weakly.

"I guess so," he replied, thinking that he needed to turn the subject to her. "But what about you? What are the doctors saying?"

"They say I will be here at least a couple of more days. I just hate to be in here instead of helping you figure out this mess. I am so happy for you." Pressley smiled, clearly weak and exhausted. Turning her head to Douglas, she thanked him and Doris for taking care of her home and chickens while she was hospitalized. Pressley was fading fast, and Doris insisted that everyone leave so Pressley could rest.

*****

Ham radio was a favorite way for Jesper to pass the time and had been a hobby since his father taught him. He had not recently taken the time to engage himself further in this hobby, but he decided now was a good time to do so. He and both his parents had earned their ham radio licenses the year before his parents died. The test to obtain a license wasn't something everyone could pass, but with his mental acuity, passing the test had been easy. A battered antenna still hovered above the roof of his blue stucco and was considered a major eyesore by all members of the Historical Society. In fact, the antenna had been a top agenda of recent meetings.

Most neighbors were willing to tolerate the appearance; some shook their heads visibly in disapproval, and others tried their best not to look as they passed by his place. Jesper picked up the microphone and turned on the radio, choosing "scan" mode.

Jess sat with the microphone in his hand, thinking of all the events that had happened within the last couple of months and all the yet-unanswered questions that had been raised. Cammie was due to come over for a late dinner after her shift, and he was thinking of inviting her to stay over, but he hadn't decided yet whether that was a good idea. One thought led to another: What would the doctors eventually conclude had happened to Pressley?

Anti had been dropped off at his place, and she was still running from room to room to refamiliarize herself with these surroundings. Jesper smiled down at Anti as she wagged her tail and looked up. Since she was a puppy, Pressley and Jesper had shared care of Anti whenever the Dyers went on their trips to buy new antiques for their store. Anti seemed to be asking what was next. Either that, or she was asking for her third breakfast.

Anti sat on her back legs and began to beg more diligently. Jesper gave her a dog biscuit and answered her seeming query. "We will have to see, Anti. We will have to see!" he said, turning to the scanner to seek friendly voices. "There is going to be a *new* Beach Reed. That seems for sure. Around here, whatever happens next is likely to be a regular curiosity!"

The author is a retired registered nurse. She lives with her husband, daughter, two dogs, chickens, turtles, and other pocosin-dwelling creatures in the beautiful country environment of Council, North Carolina.